LET ME BE FRANK WITH YOU

LET ME BE FRANK WITH YOU

A FRANK BASCOMBE BOOK

RICHARD FORD

BLOOMSBURY

LONDON · NEW DELHI · NEW YORK · SYDNEY

First published in Great Britain 2014

Copyright © 2014 by Richard Ford

The moral right of the author has been asserted

Bloomsbury Publishing Plc
50 Bedford Square
London
WC1B 3DP

www.bloomsbury.com

Bloomsbury is a trademark of Bloomsbury Publishing Plc

Bloomsbury Publishing, London, New Delhi, New York and Sydney

A CIP catalogue record for this book is available from the British Library

ISBN 978 1 4088 5348 1 (hardback edition)
ISBN 978 1 4088 5349 8 (trade paperback edition)

10 9 8 7 6 5 4 3 2 1

Designed by Suet Yee Chong
Printed and bound in Great Britain by CPI Group (UK) Ltd, Croydon CR0 4YY

ALSO BY RICHARD FORD

A Piece of My Heart (1976)
The Ultimate Good Luck (1981)
The Sportswriter (1986)
Rock Springs (1987)
Wildlife (1990)
Independence Day (1995)
Women With Men: Three Stories (1997)
A Multitude of Sins (2002)
The Lay of the Land (2006)
Canada (2012)

Kristina

CONTENTS

I'm Here

STRANGE FRAGRANCES RIDE THE TWITCHY, wintry air at The Shore this morning, two weeks before Christmas. Flowery wreaths on an ominous sea stir expectancy in the unwary.

It is, of course, the bouquet of large-scale home repair and re-hab. Fresh-cut lumber, clean, white PVC, the lye-sniff of Sakrete, stinging sealants, sweet tar paper, and denatured spirits. The starchy zest of Tyvek mingled with the ocean's sulfurous weft and Barnegat Bay's landward stink. It is the air of full-on disaster. To my nose—once practiced in these things—nothing smells of ruin as fragrantly as the first attempts at rescue.

I notice it first at the red light at Hooper Ave., and then again when I gas up my Sonata at the Hess, before heading to the bridge, Toms River to Sea-Clift. Here in the rich gas-station scents, a wintry breeze flitters my hair while my dollars spool along like a slot machine in the gathering

December clouds. Breeze has set the silver whirly-gigs to spinning at the Grandly Re-Opened Bed Bath & Beyond at the Ocean County Mall ("Only new bedding can keep us down"). Across its acres of parking, a tenth full at ten A.M., the Home Depot—Kremlin-like, but enigmatically-still-your-friend-in-spite-of-all—has thrown its doors open wide and early. Customers trail out, balancing boxes of new toilet works, new motherboards, new wiring harnesses, shrink-wrapped hinge assemblies, hollow-core doors, an entire front stoop teetering on a giant shopping cart. All is on its way to some still-standing domicile blotto'd by the hurricane—six weeks past, but not lost from memory. Everyone's still stunned here—quarrelsome, funked, put-upon-but-resolute. All are committed to "coming back."

Out here, under the Hess awning, someone's piped in loud, sports-talk radio for us customers—the *Pat 'n' Mike Show* from Magic 107 in Trenton. I was once among their faithful. They're old now. A booming voice—it's Mike—declares, "Wowee, Patrick. Coach Benziwicki cut loose quite a hurricane of F-BOMBS, I'm telling you. A real thirty-seconds-over-Tokyo."

"Let's listen to it again," Pat says, through a speaker built deep inside the gas pump. "Total disbelief. *To*-tal. This was on *ESPN!*"

Another gravelly, exhausted, recorded voice—Coach

B's—takes up, in a fury: "Okay. Let me just tell you so-called F-BOMB sportswriters one F-BOMB thing. Okay, you F-BOMBS? When *you* can F-BOMB coach a team of nine-year-old F-BOMB grammar school girls, then I might, *might* give you one shred of F-BOMB respect. Until then, you F-BOMBS, you can DOUBLE F-BOMB yourselves from here to F-BOMB Sunday dinner. You heard it here first."

The vacant-eyed, white-suited young Hess attendant who's pumping my gas hears nothing. He looks at me as if I wasn't here.

"That about says it all, I guess," Mike concedes.

"And *then* some," Pat concurs. "Just drop your keys on the desk, Coach. You're done. Take the F-BOMB *bus* back to F-BOMB Chillicothe."

"Un-F-BOMB-believable."

"Let's pause for a break, you F-BOMB."

"Me? You're the F-BOMB. Ha-ha-ha. Ha-ha-ha-ha."

IN RECENT WEEKS, I'VE BEGUN COMPILING A PER-sonal inventory of words that, in my view, should no longer be usable—in speech or *any* form. This, in the belief that life's a matter of gradual subtraction, aimed at a solider, more-nearly-perfect essence, after which all mentation goes and we head off to our own virtual Chillicothes. A reserve of fewer, better words could help, I think, by setting an example for clearer thinking. It's not so different from moving to Prague and not learning the language, so that the English you end up speaking to make yourself understood bears a special responsibility to be clear, simple, and value-bearing. When you grow old, as I am, you pretty much live in the accumulations of life anyway. Not that much is happening, except on the medical front. Better to strip things down. And where better to start stripping than the *words* we choose to express our increasingly rare, increasingly vagrant thoughts. It would be challenging, for instance, for a native Czech speaker to fully appreciate the words *poop* or *friggin'*, or the phrase "We're pregnant," or "What's the take-away?" Or, for that matter, *awesome* when it only means "tolerable." Or *preemie* or *mentee* or *legacy*. Or *no problem* when you really mean "You're welcome." Likewise, *soft landing, sibs, bond, hydrate* (when it just means "drink"), *make art, share, reach out, noise* used as a verb, and . . . apropos of Magic One-Oh-Seven: *F-Bomb. Fuck,* to me, is still pretty serviceable as a noun, verb, or adjective, with clear and distinct colorations to its already rich history. Language imitates the public riot, the poet said. And what's today's life *like,* if not a riot?

YESTERDAY, JUST PAST EIGHT, AN UNEXPECTED PHONE call disrupted my morning. My wife, Sally, answered but got me out of bed to talk. I'd been lying awake in the early sunlight and shadows, daydreaming about the possibility that somewhere, somehow, some good thing was going on that would soon affect me and make me happy, only I didn't know it yet. Since I took leave of the real-estate business (after decades), anticipation of this kind is the thing I keenly miss. Though it's the only thing, given how realty matters have gone and all that's happened to me. I am content here in Haddam, aged sixty-eight, enjoying the Next Level of life—conceivably the last: a member of the clean-desk demographic, freed to do unalloyed good in the world, should I choose to. In that spirit, I travel once a week up to Newark Liberty with a veterans' group, to greet the weary, puzzled, returning troopers home-cycling-in from Afghanistan and Iraq. I don't truly credit this as a "commitment" or a true "giving back," since it's hardly inconvenient to stand smiling, hand outstretched, loudly declaring, "Welcome home, soldier (or sailor or airman)! Thank you for your service!" It's more grandstanding than serious, and mostly meant to demonstrate that *we're* still relevant, and thus is guaranteed to prove we're not. In any case, my personal sensors are on alert for more I can do that's positive with my end-of-days' time—known otherwise as *retirement*.

"Frank? It's Arnie Urquhart," a gruff, male, too-loud telephone voice crackled through distant girdering, automotive-traffic noises. Somewhere in the background was music—Peter, Paul & Mary singing "Lemon Tree" from far-away '65. "Le-mun tree, ve-ry pritty / and the lemun flower is sweet . . ." Where I was standing in my pajamas, staring out the front window as the Elizabethtown Water meter-reader strode up the front walk to check on our consumption, my mind fled back to the face of ultra-sensual *Mary*—cruel-mouthed, earthy, blond hair slashing, her alto-voiced promise of no-nonsense coitus you'd renounce all dignity for, while knowing full well you wouldn't make the grade. A far cry from how she ended life years on—muu-muu'd and unrecognizable. (Which one of the other two was the weenie-waver? One moved to Maine.) " . . . but the fruit of the poor lemun is im-poss-i-bul to eat . . ."

"Turn something down, Arnie," I said through the noise-clutter to wherever Arnie was on the planet. "I can't hear you."

"Oh yeah. Okay." A slurping wind-noise of glass being powered closed. Poor Mary went silent as the stone she's buried under.

The connection was clearer, then went vacant a long moment. I don't talk to people on the phone that much anymore.

"Why do weathermen all wish for a fuckin' sunny day?" Arnie said, now at a distance from the phone. He'd put me on *speaker* and seemed to be talking out of the past.

"It's in their DNA," I said from my front window.

"Yep, yep." Arnie sighed a great rattling sigh. Cars were audibly whizzing past wherever he was.

"Where *are* you, Arnie?"

"Pulled over on the goddamned Garden State, by Cheesequake. Heading down to Sea-Clift, or whatever the fuck's left of it."

"I see," I said. "How's your house?"

"*Do* you see, Frank? Well, I'm glad you fuckin' see."

Back in the bonanza days of the now-popped realty bubble, I sold Arnie not just *a* house, but *my* house. In Sea-Clift. A tall, glass-and-redwood, architect-design beach palace, flush up against what seemed to be a benign and glimmering sea. Anybody's dream of a second home. I saw to it Arnie coughed up a pretty penny (two-point-eight, no "vig" on a private sale). Sally and I had decided to move inland. I was ready to take down my shingle. It was eight years ago, this fall—two weeks before Christmas, like now.

In my defense, I'd made several calls up to Arnie's principal residence in Hopatcong, to learn how his/my beach house had weathered the storm. I'd called several old clients, including my former realty partner. All their news was bad, bad, bad. In Haddam, Sally and I lost only two small oak saplings (one already dead), half the roof on her potting shed, plus a cracked windshield on my car. "A big nothing," as my mother used to say, before making a *pppttt* farting noise with her lips and laughing out loud.

"I called you, probably three times, Arnie," I said, feeling the curdling, giddy sensation of being a liar—though I'm not, not about this.

The Elizabethtown guy gave me the thumbs-up as he headed out to his truck. Our water usage for November—not a problem.

"That's like calling the corpse to say you're sorry he's dead." Arnie's speaker-phone voice faded out and in from Cheesequake. "What were you going to suggest, Frank? Take me to lunch? Buy your house back? There's no fuckin' house left down there, you jackass."

I didn't have an answer. Patent gestures of kindness, commiseration, fellow-feeling, shared sorrow and empathy—all are weak sisters in the fight against real loss. I'd only wanted to know the worst hadn't happened—which, I saw, it hadn't. Though Sea-Clift was where the big blow had come ashore like Dunkirk. No chance to dodge a bullet.

"I'm not blaming *you,* Frank. That's not why I'm on the blower here." Arnie Urquhart is an ancient Michigan Wolverine like me. Class of '68. Hockey. Rhodes finalist. Lambda Chi. Navy Cross. We all talked like that in those breezy, troubled days. The blower. The crapper. The Z-machine. The libes. The gazoo. Boogies. Gooks. Hogans . . . it's a wonder any of us were ever allowed to hold a paying job. Arnie owns and runs—or did—a carriage-trade seafood boutique in north Jersey and has made a mint selling shad roe, Iranian caviar, and imported Black Sea delicacies the FDA doesn't know about—all of it delivered in unidentifiable, white panel trucks—to Schlumberger execs for exclusive parties no one hears about, including President Obama, who wouldn't be invited, since in the high-roller Republicans' view, chitlins' and hog-maws wouldn't be on the menu.

"How can I help, Arnie?" I was watching the Elizabethtown truck motor away down Wilson Lane. Clients' first target of opportunity when a home sale goes sour—no matter when—is almost always the realtor, whose intentions are almost always good.

"I'm on my way down there now, Frank. Some Italian piece of shit called me up at home. Wants to buy the lot and the house—whatever's left of it—for five hundred grand. I need some advice. You got any?" More cars whizzing.

"I'm not using any of mine, Arnie," I said. "What's the situation down there?"

I, of course, knew. We'd all seen it on CNN, then seen it and seen it and seen it 'til we didn't care anymore. Nagasaki-by-the-sea—with the Giants and Falcons just a tempting channel click away.

"You'll get a kick out of it, Frank," Arnie said, disembodied in his car. "Where is it you live now?"

"Haddam." Sally had come to the door from the kitchen in her yoga clothes, holding a tea mug to her lips, breathing steam away, looking at me as if she'd heard something distressing and I should possibly hang up.

A loud truck-horn blare cracked the silence where Arnie was. "Ass Hole," Arnie shouted. "Haddam. Okay. Nice place. Or it was once." Arnie bumped something against the speaker. "My house—*your* house—is sixty yards inland now, Frank. On its side—if it had a side. The neighbors are all worse off. The Farlows tried to ride it out in their safe room. They're goners. The Snedikers made a run for it at the last minute. Ended up in the bay. Barb and I were at Lake Sunapee at my son's. We watched it. I saw my house on TV before I saw it in person."

"I guess that could be good news."

Arnie didn't respond.

"What d'you want me to do, Arnie?"

"I'm driving down to meet the cocksuckers. *Flip* companies. You heard of them? Speculators." Arnie had started speaking in some kind of tough-guy, Jersey gangster growl.

"I heard about them." I'd read about it all in the *Times*.

"So you see the whole deal. I need your advice, Frank. You used to be honest."

"I've been out of the realty business a while, Arnie. My license is expired. All I know is what I read in the newspaper."

"It'll make you more reliable. Take away the profit motive. I'm not planning to shoot you, if you're worried about that."

"I hadn't quite gotten to there, Arnie." Though I had. It had already happened. Once in Ortley Beach, once in Sea Girt. Listing agents shot sitting at their desks, typing out offer sheets.

"So. Are you gonna show up? I could say you owe me." Another truck's withering horn went blasting past. "Jesus. These fucks. *I'm* gonna get killed out here. So?"

"Okay, I'll come," I said, just to get Arnie off the road shoulder and on to the scene of destruction.

"Eleven o'clock tomorrow. At the house," Arnie said. "Or where it used to be. You *might* recognize it. I'm driving a silver Lexus."

"I'll be there."

"Are we gonna have NHL this year, Frank?" Hockey. Destruction's great leveler.

"I haven't really kept up, Arnie."

"The shit-for-brains players," Arnie said. "They got the best deal they'll ever get. Now they'll have to settle for less. Sound familiar?" As always, Arnie was on management's side. "Hail to the Victors, Frank."

"Champions of the West, Arnie."

"Mañana en la mañana." Which seemed to be how Arnie said thanks.

OUT ON LITTLE LEAGUE WORLD CHAMPIONS BOU-levard, Toms River, nothing looks radically changed storm-wise. In a purely retinal sense, the barrier island across the bay has done its god-given work for the inland communities, though much lies in ruins here, back in the neighborhoods. Traffic is anemic along the once–Miracle Mile, headed toward the bridge. It's plain, though, that Toms River has claimed some survivor's cred. A beardless Santa sits on a red plastic milk crate in front of the Launch Pad coffee hut (he's clearly a Mexican), a red, printed-cardboard sign resting against his knee. COFFEE GIVES YOU COURAGE. FELIZ NAVIDAD. I wave, but he only stares back, as if I might be giving him the finger. Farther on, the Free At Last Bail Bonds has only a single car parked in front, as do a couple of boxy, asbestos-sided bars set back in the gravel lots. Days were—before The Shore got re-discovered and prices went nuts—you could drive over from Pottstown, take the kids and your honeybee for a weekend, and get away for a couple hundred. All that's a dream now, even after the storm. A big sign—part of its message torn off by the winds—advertises the Glen Campbell Good-bye Tour. Half of Glen's smiling, too-handsome face remains, a photo from the '60s—before Tanya and the boozing and the cocaine. A paper placard in front of one of the bars—stolen off someone's lawn after the election—has been re-purposed and instead of "Obama-Biden" now announces, "We're Back. So Fuck You, Sandy."

Driving, I've got Copland's *Fanfare* filling the interior space at ten thirty. I bought the whole oeuvre online. As always, I'm stirred by the opening oboes giving ground to the strings then the kettle drums and the double basses. It's a high-sky morning in Wyoming. Joel McCrea's galloping across a windy prairie. Barbara Britton, fresh from Vermont, stands out front of their sodbuster cabin. *Why is he so late? Is there trouble? What can I do, a woman alone?* I've worn out three disks this fall. Almost any Copland (today it's the Pittsburgh Symphony conducted by some Israeli) can persuade me on almost any given day that I'm not just any old man doing something old men do: driving to the grocery for soy milk, visiting the periodontist, motoring to the airport to greet young soldiers—sometimes against their wills. It doesn't take much to change my perspective on a given day—or a given moment, or a given anything. Sally slipped a Copland in my Christmas stocking a year ago (*Billy the*

Kid), and it's had positive effects. I bought *The Tibetan Book of Living and Dying* as a present to myself but haven't made much progress there—though I need to.

I haven't had time to look up Arnie Urquhart's home-sale paperwork from '04—whether he financed, if he took a balloon, or just peeled bills off a fat wad. I, of course, ought to remember the transaction, since it was *my* house, and I pocketed the dough—used to finance our house in Haddam, with plenty left over. Though like a lot of things I should do, I often don't. It's not true that as you get older things slide away like molasses off a table top. What *is* true is I don't remember some things that well, owing to the fact that I don't care all that much. I now wear a cheap Swatch watch, but I do sometimes lose the handle on the day of the month, especially near the end and the beginning, when I get off-track about "thirty days hath September . . ." This, I believe, is normal and doesn't worry me. It's not as if I put my trousers on backwards every morning, tie my shoelaces together, and can't find my way to the mailbox. My only persistent bother is an occasionally painful subluxation (a keeper word) in my C-3 and C-4. It causes me to feel "Rice Krispies" in my neck, plus an ache when I twist back and forth, so that I don't do that as much. I fear it may be restricting signals to my brain. My orthopedist at Haddam Medical, Dr. Zippee (a Pakistani and a prime asshole), asked if I wanted him to order up "some blood work" to find out if I'm a candidate for Alzheimer's. (It made him glee-ful to suggest this.) "Thanks, but I guess not," I said, standing in his tiny green cubicle in a freezing-ass, flower-print exam-ination gown. "I'm not sure what I'd do with the information." "You'd probably forget it," he said, gloating. He's also told me that a usually unobserved vertical crease down the earlobe is a "good marker" for heart disease. I, of course, have one, though it isn't deep—which I hope is a positive sign.

My view of the "Big A," though—should I ever have it—is that it quickly becomes its own comfort zone and is not as bad as it's billed. Dr. Zippee, who attended med school in Karachi and interned down at Hopkins, travels back to the old country every winter to work in a madrassa (whatever that is). He complains to me that America, in its vengeful zeal to run the world, has ruined life where he came from; that the Tali-ban started out as good guys who were on our side. But now, thanks to us, the streets aren't safe at night. I tell him, to me Pakistanis and Indians are the same people, like Israelis and Arabs, and northern and southern Irishmen. Religion's just their excuse to maim and incinerate each other—otherwise they'd die of boredom. "Awesome," he says and laughs like a chimp. He's recently bought a cottage on Mount Desert and hopes soon to leave New Jersey behind. In his view, life is about pain management, and I need to do a better job man-aging mine.

Copland's soaring as I make it out onto the bridge. Barnegat Bay, this morning, is a sea of sequins the wind plays over, with the long island and Seaside Heights out ahead, appearing, in a moment of spearing sunlight, to be unchanged. Gulls are towering. A few tiny numbered sails are dimpling far out on a gusty land breeze. The temperature's topped out at thirty-five. You'd need to be a show-off to be on the water. I'm certain I'm dressed too lightly, though I'm elated to be back at The Shore, even to face disaster. Our true emotions are never conventional.

An Air-Tran—one of the old vibrator 737s—is just nosing up from Atlantic City into the low, gray ceiling, full of sleepy gamblers, headed back to Milwaukee. I can make out the lowercase "a" on its tail, as it disappears into the fog off the ocean side where my old house once sat, but apparently sits no more.

Later yesterday morning, after I spoke to Arnie, Sally came downstairs to where I was eating my All-Bran, and stood staring, musing through the window into the back yard at the late-autumn squirrel activity. I was pleased to be thinking nothing worth recording, not about Arnie Urquhart, just breathing to the cadence of my chews. After a while of not speaking, she sat down across from me, holding a book I'd noticed her reading late into the night—her light stayed on after I'd gone to sleep, then was switched off, then on again later. It's not unusual for people our age.

"I read this shocking thing last night." She held the book she'd been engrossed by, clutched to her yoga shirt. Her eyes were intent. She seemed worried. I couldn't make out the book's spine but understood she meant to tell me about it.

"Tell me," I said.

"Well." She pursed her lips. "Back in 1862, right when the Civil War was in full swing, the U.S. Cavalry had time to put down an Indian revolt in Minnesota. Did you know that?"

"I did," I said. "The Dakota uprising. It's pretty famous."

"Okay. You know about it. I didn't."

"I know *some* things," I said and stared down at a banana slice.

"Okay. But. In December of 1862, our government hanged thirty-eight Sioux warriors on one big scaffold. Just did it all at once."

"That's famous, too," I said. "Supposedly they'd massacred eight hundred white people. Not that *that's* an excuse."

Sally took in a breath and turned her head away in a manner to indicate a tear she didn't want seen might be wobbling out of her eyes. "But do you know what they said?" These words were nearly choked with throat-clogging emotion.

"What *who* said?"

"The Indians. They all began shouting out as they were standing on the gallows, waiting to drop and never speak again."

I didn't know. But I looked up to let her understand I realized this was important to her, and that the next thing she said would be important to me. Possibly my spoon had paused on its upward arc toward my mouth. I may have shaken my head in amazement.

"They all shouted, 'I'm here!' They started calling that out in their Sioux language, all around that awful contraption that was about to kill them. People who heard it said it was awe-inspiring." (Not awesome.) "No one ever forgot it. Then they hanged them. All of them. At one moment. 'I'm here.' As if that made it all right for them. Made death tolerable and less awful. It gave them strength." Sally shook her head. Her tear of anguish for long-ago 1862 did not emerge. She held her book tight to her front and smiled at me mournfully, across the glass-topped table where I've eaten possibly three thousand breakfasts. "I just thought you'd want to know about that. I'm sorry to ruin your breakfast."

"I'm glad to know about it, sweetheart," I said. "It didn't ruin my breakfast at all."

"I'm here," she said and seemed to embarrass herself.

"So am I," I said.

And with those words she got up, came around the square

table, kissed me once on my forehead, still embarrassed, then went away, carrying her book back to where she'd come from in the house.

Midway on the bridge, headed across to darkest Seaside Heights, where who knows what awaits me (heart-strings plucked, outrage, wronged rectitude, and all that's right corrupted), I realize there's nothing I can really do for Arnie Urquhart's domiciliary suffering, or to make things jake. Jake's already blown out the window and all but forgotten, from what I've seen on TV. And yet: you bear *some* responsibility to another human you sell a house to. Not a financial one. Conceivably not a moral one. But one in which, even rarer, the professional and human operate on a single set of rails. A priestly, vocational responsibility. Though for all I know, Arnie might just as easily feel *relief* that his house is an ass-over-teacups total loss. It may have been just the thing he'd lain in bed and dreamed about—like the day you sell your vintage, lap-sided Lyman in-board: the runner-up best day of your life, after the day you bought it. Second-house ownership is often like that. People know they're going to rue the day long before they sign the papers—but they do it anyway. Arnie may just be pretending to mourn. After all, he now owns a hunk of prime, undeveloped oceanfront—even if the taxes stay high. He can sit tight and wait for destiny—assuming anybody ever wants oceanfront again.

Though what I sense with my ex-realtor's brain is that Arnie may simply want me to take the trouble to be there—to be his witness. It's what the Christers all long for, dawn to dusk. It's why there are such things as "best men," "pallbearers," "godfathers," "invitees to an execution." Everything's more real if two can see it. A flying saucer. A Sasquatch. The face of the Redeemer in an oil smear at Jiffy Lube. And today I'm willing to say "I'm here" to whoever can hear me, and for whatever good it might do for man or beast.

An unusual sight greets me as I curve down off the bridge into what used to be Seaside Heights (Central Ave., north to Ortley Beach, south to Sea-Clift). A New Jersey State Police command-post trailer has been hauled across the roadway to block unauthorized vehicles. Sawhorses are piled against Jersey barriers, red and silver flashers spinning on a striped trooper car that's parked alongside—everything but razor wire and a machine-gun nest—beyond which the wound of the storm's destruction assaults my eye. Up Central, toward my old office, as far as I can see along the beach side of the avenue, civic life has sustained a fierce whacking—house roofs sheared off, exterior walls stripped away, revealing living rooms full of furniture, pictures on bed tables, closets stuffed with clothes, stoves and refrigerators standing out *white* for all to see. Other houses are simply gone altogether. Great, heaping Mount Trashmores (one with a Christmas tree on top), piled with building debris, dirt, sand, ruined Halloween decorations, auto fenders, cabinets, toilets, mailboxes—all that could be bashed into and blown to smithereens—have risen on every corner. Awaiting *what,* it's not clear. Meanwhile, a god's own lot of human activity's underway beneath the mottled sky, up the avenue and down the side-leading residential streets, ocean to bay. Much of it, I see, is police activity—large men in SWAT-team garb, and National Guard troopers in desert issue, their tiny lethal riflery strapped to their chests, patrolling. There are State Health vans with workers in white hazmat suits. Power-line people are here with cherry pickers (they come in convoys from Texas and Minnesota, and won't be kept away). As well, there're trucks of every species— Datsuns like the terrorists in Kabul use, new F-150s, raised Dodge muscle rigs, all the way to elephant-size dumpers and decommissioned garbage scows—conscripted to get destruction, pain, the memory of pain and destruction, up, out and away and into some landfill in Elizabeth like the 9/11 remains. Nothing's livable or OPEN. There's no power. A carpet of ocean and beach sand has been driven up onto the streets and yards and under all the ruined cars, as if The Shore in a single night had turned into Riyadh. It's a post-combat zone, though in its own way perfectly pacific and orderly. I expect to see buzzards circling in the misty air. Though instead, a squadron of brown pelicans floats along the beachfront, seeking something familiar or edible or both.

In all, there's the palpable, ghostly urge to "put back" what was. Though, in my view—just arriving—it's too bad it can't be left as it is a bit longer, like a ghost that goes on spooking. Decades ago, in my unsatisfactory Marine Corps tour, a few of us privates were dispatched as forward observers from Camp Pendleton down to Ensenada, to surveil enemy buildup in the local bordellos and mescalerias. At the time, I noticed it was impossible to discern if the tumbled-down Mexican buildings we passed were actually tumbled down or half tumbled *up,* with new residents waiting somewhere offstage. Ortley Beach—what I can see of it now—looks that way, as I'm sure do all the once-sparkling beach towns north and south: locked into a moment of indecisiveness between being and not being. I once made a handsome living off this patch of now-salted earth. I should be able to envision the grains of possibility in what's left of it. But for the moment, I cannot.

LOOTERS BEWARE! A SIGN ON THE SHOULDER OF THE exit curve warns all who'd enter and do ill. A skull 'n' crossbones has been painted on in red to drive the point home. CURFEW 6 PM THIS MEANS U! fills out the space to make it personal. A forest of other signs is sprouted around like political yard art, announcing, WE'LL BUY YOUR HOUSE (OR WHAT'S LEFT OF IT). MARTELLO BROTHERS—REFUSE HAULING. HABLA INGLES—RAPIDO! LEARN GRIEF COUNSELING IN TEN DAYS. FAST MOLD REMOVAL. KNOW YOUR RIGHTS. WRITERS' COOPERATIVE. NRA ICE-BREAKER AT THE TOMS RIVER HAMPTON INN. A DRUNK DRIVER KILLED MY DAUGHTER. FLOW YOGA. TANTRIC SEX WORKSHOP. FIRST RESPONDERS SPAGHETTI SUPPER. One sign merely says NOTHING BESIDE REMAINS (for victims with a liberal arts degree).

As I nose up to the command-post trailer, Copland turned off, a policeman steps out a side door down to the sandy pavement. No one's permitted in except contractors, owners, and local officialdom (plus President Obama and our big candied yam of a governor). But I'm in luck. The cop, hiking up his heavy cop belt and situating his blue hat on his big cop head, is a man I know. It is Corporal Alyss of the Sea-Clift PD. Years back, I sold his house in Seaside Park when he was a rookie and his family size suddenly doubled, requiring a bigger, cheaper place—in Silverton.

Palm forward, Officer Alyss transforms himself now into a human Jersey-barrier, warning off looters, unauthorized rubberneckers, and sneakers-in like me. When I buzz down my window, he comes round to utter his discouraging words, big right hand rested on his big black Glock. He's much larger than the last time I saw him. Portland concrete seems to have been added to his shape and size, in-uniform. He doesn't quite move naturally—fully Kevlar'd with heavy, combat footwear as thick as moon boots, plus his waist-harness of black-leather cop gear: scorch-your-eyes perpetrator spray, silver cuffs, a walkie-talkie as big as a textbook, a head-knocking baton in a metal loop, extra ammo clips, a row of black snap-closed compartments that could hold most anything, plus a pair of sinister black gloves. He is the Michelin man of first respond-ers, his police ball cap with gold insignia beetled down to his eyebrows. I want to laugh, since he's a sweetie at heart. But he's too uncomfortable not to be sympathized with. In any case, laughing at the police is a prime misstep in New Jersey.

"Okay, sir. I just need you to . . ." Corporal Alyss begins his "just-turn-'er-around-and-head-your-ass-on-back-across-the bridge" spiel. As I suspected, he's not seen me properly. Though a sneaky smile's awakening, and he shifts his big face to the side, leaning toward my window, like a kid (a big kid). "All right. *All* right," he says, his smile breaking through, becoming in an instant the jolliest of gendarmes. I'm outed as a friendly. (He takes plenty of ribbing about his name—Alyss/Alice—and has clearly grown into his job.) His big Ukrainian earlobes, I notice—fat, pendulous, and pink—do not have the hint of a crease. He obviously lacks a care in the world. All his needs are met with his tidy Silverton family, a badge, and a gun. "I guess you're down here to teach us all how smart you are to get out when you did," he says. He's beaming, his big, blue Slavic eyes wide and intense as he peers in and around inside my car. He is only thirty-five, played tight end at Rider, then spent a year in Ecuador on his Pentecostal mission, bullying the natives into accepting Jesus. His old man was a beat cop in Newark and paid "the ultimate price." You get to know such things in the realty business. His wife, Berta, was one of the nurses who looked after me when I got shot and stayed a long time in the hospital.

"I'm just going down to counsel an old client, Pete. His house got blown away." No need to tell him it was *my* house. Just the facts, here.

"Yeah, well, tell me about it," Corporal Alyss says, his smile fading. He is not a handsome boy—all his features way too big, too pink, too fleshy—a cross between a Minnesota farmer and one of his animals. He's lucky to have a wife. His little shoulder microphone sputters, but emits no voice. Even though he might not say it—and though he himself moved years ago—it probably rankles him that I moved away. "Your old office is an empty lot," he says. "Back wall just blew in." He's all police business-y now, as if some training session he's sat through has flashed up into his thick head. Our friendship is paling.

"I heard," I say up through the window. Chill air has rushed in, carrying sour odors of ocean and diesel and Corporal A's leather rigging. Another cop, a black, hatless NJ state trooper in jodhpurs, has appeared at the trailer door, watching us gravely. He takes note of my license plate, then steps back inside, where they're probably playing hearts. "Did you guys survive okay," by which I mean him and his brood.

"Just lost our electric. Some roof coping," he says soberly, extending his lip. "Nothing like down here. Insurance won't pay ours either, though. Ours is supposedly wind, not water." He inserts a big thumb knuckle into his ear canal for a scratch, cocks his mouth awry, while his other hand rests on his police issue. He's most at ease not moving. "The wife's having repetitive thought patterns. Just worrying, you know?" He's forgotten I know her and know her name. All is policing to police. The rest of the world is like groceries on the shelf.

"I guess it's natural."

"Oh yeah." He looks confident and says nothing more, as he thinks about what's "natural" and what's not.

"Okay if I drive on down to Poincinet Road?" I try to act like I've already been there twenty times and am going back to resume whatever I was doing before.

"That's all changed down there," he said. "The storm, *and* before the storm. You prolly won't recognize it. But yeah. Just be careful." He takes his thumb out of his ear and wipes his nose with it, then backs away from my car door. He produces a tiny red notebook from his flak-vest pocket, and with a ballpoint notes down my license number. "I'll write you down in case you get in there, and we never see you again. We'll know who to call." He smiles at his note-taking. He is a mystery—even for all that's plain about him. It's not easy to balance his life: one minute friendly; one minute a hostage situation; and all the time in between longing to be home with the kids, cooking *brats* on the Weber and smiling at the day.

"Great," I say. "I'll be safe."

"No worries." (. . . On my inventory; a two-word misnomer meaning "You're absolutely welcome. I'm really glad to be able to assist you. After all, we seek each other in these dire times. So know that I'm thinking about you. And do be safe.") *No worries* is maybe better.

I run my window back up. Corporal Alyss steps farther back, drags the NJSP sawhorse to the left, waves me through past the skull 'n' bones and the message from Ozymandias. I give him my two-hand fellowship wave and drive on. His back is already to me. He's forgetting I exist. I'm here. He's here. But, in another sense, we're not.

SEA-CLIFT, WHEN I DRIVE SOUTH ON CENTRAL, gives to the world the sad look of having taken a near-fatal punch in the nose. Power poles are mostly up but lacking wires. Sand has eddied up over everything low-down. Houses—even the now-and-then ones that look unscathed—seem stunned to stillness. Roofs, windows, front stoops, exterior walling, garages, boats shrink-wrapped in blue polypropylene—all look as if a giant has strode out of the gray sea and kicked the shit out of everything. Here are all places where people have *lived*. And not just smarty-pants, foggy-shuttered summer renters who stay ninety days past Memorial Day, but a sturdy corps of old-time "Clift-dwellers" plus happy retirees, alongside an older echelon of hedge-fund, coupon clippers who've bought in since the '70s and call it "home." Each in his own way patronizes the pizzerias, the mom-and-pops, the car-repairs, the Chinese takeout, the fried-seafood eateries where the TV's never off in the bar and a booth's always waiting. A bracing atmosphere of American faux egalitarianism long has reigned here—which drew me two decades back, when I moved down from Haddam. I arrived when seven hundred thousand still meant seven hundred thousand and could buy you a piece of heaven. With Sally Caldwell as my helpmate I couldn't have been happier.

All *that* life has now been poleaxed and strewn around like hay-straw, so that even a hardened disaster-tourist who sees opportunity in everything would have to ask himself: "What can you do with this now? Let it settle back to nature?

Walk away and come back in a year or ten? Move to Nova Scotia? Shoot yourself?"

Here, too, the morning's bustling with cleanup-removal-and-teardown, line re-stringing, front-loader and backhoe operations. Citizens are about—though many are just standing, hands-on-hips staring at their ruined abodes. As Corporal Alyss has said, it's easy to see how a person could drive down on a reconnoitering mission and simply never show up again; as if calamity had left a hole in the world on the rim of which everything civilized and positive-tending teeters— spirits, efforts, hopes, dreams, memories . . . buildings, for sure—all in jeopardy of spiraling down and down. I *do,* in fact, feel smart for having gotten out when the getting was good. Though when you sell a house where you've been happy, it's never that you're smart. In all such moves one feels the bruise of defeat.

At the end of Central, where my house sat, there was never an actual street, just a sign—Poincinet Road—and a rough beachfront sand track and five large, grandfathered residences, with the ocean and pearlescent beach stretching out front, the way you'd dream it. Nothing between you and paradise but fucking Portugal. It's now become an actual street—or *had* been before the climatological shit train pulled in. I see no sign of Arnie or his Lexus as I turn down the sanded-over asphalt. Though as attested, my former home, number seven—once a tall, light-strewn, board 'n' batten 'n' glass beach dazzler—lies startlingly up to the left (not right), washed backwards off its foundation, boosted topsy-turvy across the asphalt, turned sideways, tupped on its side against the grassy-sandy beach berm, and (by water, wind, and the devil's melee) ridded of its roof. Its back-side exterior wall where I once entered through a red door (gone) is stripped of its two-car garage and torn free of interior fittings (pipes, re-bar, electric), the dangling filaments of which along with whatever else ever connected it to the rest of the world, hanging limp from the house's exposed "bottom," which you used not to be able to see. The blond-brick chimney's gone— though not the stone fireplace, which I can make out in the ripped-open living room. The banistered outside steps have disappeared. The panoramic deck, where I spent happy nights gazing at constellations I couldn't identify, is bent down and clinging to the broken superstructure by lug bolts I dutifully tightened each fall. What was then glass is now gaping. Studs show through the "open plan" where, in years past, transpired sweet, murmurous late nights with Sally, or merry drinks' evenings with some old Michigan chum who'd shown up unexpected with a bottle of Pouilly-Fuissé . . . where life went on, in other words.

The poured gray foundation is what's left intact—a sur-prisingly small rectangular pit with a partial set of wooden steps going nowhere. The big Trane heat pump's in place in the dank water that's collected. But everything else in the "basement"—bicycles, hope chests, old uniforms, generations of shoes, wine racks, busted suitcases someone's father owned, boxes and boxes and boxes of stuff you should've gotten rid of decades ago—all that's been sucked up and blown away to some farmer's field in Lakehurst, to be found, possibly returned, or else put in a museum to commemorate the awesomeness of mother nature when she gets it in her head to fuck with you.

All four other houses down Poincinet are simply missing, leaving *only* vacant cellars like my old place. Though opening up the space these houses so recently occupied has reconfigured a new pretty vista—ocean and beach the way they used to be, time immemorial. A lone fisherman in hip waders is visible, casting for stripers with his long pole to the incoming tide. He's dressed in a bulky cable-knit, heavy gloves, and an orange watch cap, and doesn't seem to have caught anything. Out at sea, between the land and the fog bank, an unmeasurable distance from where I'm sitting behind the wheel, a great white cruise ship—a wallowing twelve-decker—sits motionless against the gray. Carnival, Princess, Norwegian—one of those. I have a feeling passengers are at the rails, scoping out what used to be New Jersey, taking snaps with their phones and shooting them back to Ashtabula and Boise, as they ply their way toward Great Abaco. I'm not so certain they're empathetic to our lives ashore.

I, though, am struck by something I've never thought before—even in my role as residential specialist, seeking shelter for those in need. And it is . . . what little difference a house makes once it's gone. How effortlessly, almost sweetly, the world re-asserts its claim and becomes itself again. People wring their hands and cry bloody murder when a garish new structure rises and casts its ugly shadow; or when a parking lot behind the Pathway paves over the sacred midden of the lost Lenape or a wetland where herons nested and ducks stopped to rest. As if these evils last forever. They don't. All may not be vanity (though plenty is); but nothing's here to stay. There's something to be said for a good no-nonsense hurricane, to bully life back into perspective. It's always worthy of our notice when we don't feel precisely the way we thought we would. Easy to say, of course, since I don't live here anymore.

Up the beach, opened by the absence of what were people's houses, the sight line stretches all the way up to Ortley Beach and beyond, to where the old roller-coaster bones sit marooned in seawater. Two tiny, faraway figures are walking a dog along the surf's lap. A front loader—I hear its distant beeping through my open window—is slowly returning sand to the beach from the blanketed streets. I hear—over the berm, out of sight—the clatter of hammers striking wood, and the cheerful hum of Spanish. How strange life is. One day Reynoso, the next Sea-Clift. "Oh, jes," one of them shouts (they're English speakers now). "It's cunt sniff." At least I think that's what the words say. Frolicsome musical notes rise from their radio and over the berm top. They're gutting or hauling or de-molding someone's dream home, no doubt wearing surgical masks and rubber gloves against the spores. "*Sí, sí, sí pero. Hees* husband *ees* a Navy SEAL." "*Pendejo!*" someone answers. "Sex can't be *zhat* good. *Comprendes?*" They all laugh. Good luck is infectious.

But where's Arnie? Am I stood up? About to be ambushed from a Lexus parked at a distance? People distrust realtors in a climate of disaster. We're wildcards in the human deck, always filling out a winning hand. Though not me. Not now.

My stomach, however, has begun skirling around and ker-clunking. I should've bought cashews back at the Hess. It's almost eleven. My All-Bran is barely recollectable. I put a stick of spearmint in my mouth and let it calm things. Whether you wear falsies or not (I don't), whether you've been eating garlic or onions or pizza or *choucroute garnie* and brush your teeth eight times a day, being "older" makes you worry that you reek like a monkey's closet. Sally assures me I don't, that she'd give me "the signal." But if the machine's winding down, its parts start to fester. I've lately begun brushing my tongue morning, noon, and night, since the tongue's the petri dish for every sort of rankness. In general, it's fair to say that as you get older you experience a complexer relationship with the ongoing—which seems at odds with how it should be.

I wait in my car, chewing, beside the ruins of my house. There's no reading matter available. I've left the *Times* at home. Here's only a pamphlet Dr. Zippee amusedly gave me, depicting the exercise routine for relieving movement-inhibiting neck pain. Cartoons show a little round-headed stick figure rotating his bubble head and smiling to exhibit the golden way to neck happiness. In other squares he's displaying a mouth-down frown to show the "wrong way"—that leads to traction, invasive surgery-through-the-throat, painkillers, Betty Ford, if not all the way to Rahway. I do feel new Rice Krispies at shoulder level, which makes me wrangle my neck around. Tension's the culprit; the tension of Arnie Urquhart not goddamn being here like he said he would.

The only other reading material in my car is a copy of *We Salute You,* the publication we volunteers put into the hand of each Iraq and Afghanistan returnee the moment after we shake that hand and declare "Welcome home! Thank you for your service!" *We Salute You* is a useful cache of vital information pertaining to anything the home-leave soldier might need, want, or encounter in the first six hours stateside (assuming no one's meeting him or her, as surprisingly happens much of the time). *We Salute You* is printed by a cabal of right-wing, freedom-forum loonies out in Ohio, who nonetheless manage to do a damn good job because they don't stuff *our* magazine with any of the gun-control-anti-abortion-back-to-the-stone-age bullshit they *do* put in their regular anti-Obama mail-ings. I know, because these publications came to my house, until I made a complaint with the Post Office, after which they still came, right through the election—though by now the crackpot Ohioans might've concluded their message didn't get through.

We Salute You is printed for each U.S. port of troop entry—L.A., New York–Newark, Boston, Houston, Seat-tle, even Detroit. It's twenty gray newsprint pages (an online edition's in the works) full of important phone numbers, e-mail and postal addresses for whatever geographical area the trooper or marine or airman first puts a foot down on home soil. Panic attack, suicide, drug and alcohol abuse help-line numbers are included. Veteran-friendly taxi companies. Directions to transportation hubs. Numbers to purchase a phone card. Every church you can think of, including Mus-lims, atheists, and Agnostics Anonymous. All these numbers are, of course, obtainable by anyone—though not in such an easy, free-of-charge, depoliticized format. There's also plenty of less expectable info. Clean Vietnamese massage boutiques. Outfitters for mule pack-ins to the Sierras. A clearinghouse for online sites to help you find a former girlfriend who's abandoned you. Chat-line numbers dealing with revenge issues. Private phone numbers of all U.S. congressmen and senators. Sites for how to buy Cuban cigars and condoms by the gross. There's an LGBT strength-in-numbers line. Even a number for a Socrates Death-With-Dignity support league, where psychologists with degrees from Oberlin and Macalester try to talk a soldier back from the brink while seeming to understand that death might seem the only option.

Our mission, of course, occasionally fails. One young sailor from Piscataway, three days out of Kandahar, stuffed the exhaust pipes of his Trans-Am with stolen copies of *We Salute You*'s and slipped the surly bonds in the Washington Crossing State Park parking lot—a note taped to the steering wheel saying "Here's the future. Get ready for it." There's nothing you can do when someone's ready to go, though possibly a handshake didn't hurt.

My car clock now says eleven fifteen. The striper guy is stowing his gear in his bucket and notching his hook to his rod handle. The tide's come in. He's fished with his back to the mayhem ashore as if it wasn't there.

The tiny, distant beach figures with the trotting dog alongside have come clearly into view. They turn out to be the Glucks, unsociable neighbors from when I lived here. Arthur's a defrocked Rutgers professor (plagiarism—the usual "overlookings" and "carelessnesses"). He's trudgering along with his plump wife, Allie Ann, and an all-but-immobilized, low-riding fat brown dog I'd have sworn they had ten years ago, which would make it eighteen. "Poot." The Glucks, who must be in their late eighties, are preserved not much better than their dog and are walking with old-age difficulty along the tide-narrowed beach, arms looped, chins lowered, dressed like Eskimos, leaning into each other so that they look like one lumpy human package. Are they here, I wonder, to survey the ruins? Their house has vanished. Or did they get away (like me) and buy into staged-retirement in Somerville that buses them to the Whole Foods, keeps Columbia-trained M.D.s onsite 24/7, and lets them keep their '95 Electra 'til the State takes the keys. I'd rather jump in my watery basement hole than talk to them. What rueful recognitions would glint in their beady eyes? "Oh, yes of course, Mr. Bascombe. Of course, of course, OF COURSE!" How many old acquaintances, neighbors, former teachers, fellow marines have we all caught a glimpse of in an unexpected place and dived in an alley rather than face for a second? All because: (1) We don't want to; (2) There's too much unsaid that doesn't need to be said—a Chinese wall of words that would fall on top of us and we'd die; (3) We know others feel

the very same way about *us*. We're, most of us, the last per-
sons anyone in his right mind wants to talk to on any given
day, including Christmas.

I ease down in my seat and raise my window in case the
Glucks see me. But they don't so much as glance at my car,
parked fifty meters from where their house once staunchly
stood. They plod along the empty beach like specters, their
dog at their knees. Where would they be going but back into
the fog?

And then all of a sudden, I don't want to be here anymore—at all. Whatever inland protections I've come armed
with have worn away and rendered me—a target. Of loss. Of
sadness. The thing I didn't want to be and explicitly why I
haven't ventured down here in these last weeks, and shouldn't
have now. I have these sensations more than I like to admit,
since they make me feel that something bad is closing in—
like the advance of a shadow across a square of playground
grass where I happen to be standing. When the shadow covers
the last grass blade, the air goes suddenly chill and still, and
all is up for me. Which will ultimately be only true. So who'd
blame me for feeling it now, and here?

But I'm ready to cease and desist. Being here makes me
feel guilty-without-context. Like being present when someone you know, but don't know well, all at once falls into a pit
of despair and starts blubbering, and you can't do anything

except wish the hell he or she would stop. I feel not a straw of blame for anything hereabouts, yet somehow feel implicated by everything's dilapidation and sad future. This is more than I bargained for—much more—yet doesn't seem actually to *be* anything. Just stupid, stupid, stupid. I am. Again.

Though should I just sit—motor thrumming, hoping the continental edge will re-buoy me? Should I turn on the *Fanfare* again (Obama used it for his Lincoln Memorial speech, where it worked)? Should I climb out into the foggy chill and have a poke round my old edifice, possibly spy something I left a decade back? A plastic laundry hamper? A bicycle pump with Bascombe painted on in red nail polish? What the fuck *am* I supposed to do? Anyone else would drive off. I'm worried, of course, about picking up a roof tack in my radials.

OUTSIDE MY CAR WINDOW, ARNIE URQUHART, OR A man I take to be him, stands, talking, silenced by my closed glass. (Where's the Lexus hidden?) He's pointing beyond the berm and the ruin of my old house—his old house—a stack of sticks rained down from the sky. Conceivably I've fallen into a carbon monoxide fugue. Has he been here long? Have we had our meeting already? Have I made everything right by him, the way I once did?

Arnie seems to me to be talking about the Twin Towers,

which is possibly why he's pointing north. I used to believe I could see them from my deck, though it was only clouds and light playing tricks. "It must've taken some real nuts to do that," Arnie's saying, as I lower my window. We're suddenly very close to each other. "That huge skyscraper just coming right at you, three hundred miles a fuckin' hour. Fascinating, really." I can't open my door because Arnie's in the way. A current of damp, foggy ocean air sifts around me where I've been warm in here. When I was in college in Ann Arbor, I loved the cold. But no more. "We bring our disasters down to our own level, don't we, Frank," Arnie's saying. "But those poor people really couldn't. So we're lucky down here in a way. You know?" Arnie turns toward the wrecked corpse of his house. "Remember that place? Boy, oh boy." Out of the ocean's hiss, a foghorn moans. Surprising it would be working when nothing else is.

"Nature always has another thing to do to us, I guess, Arnie." It's my best go-to Roethke line and fits most human situations. Arnie and I traded stories about poor old Ted when I sold him the house.

"Take the lively air, Frank." Arnie says and begins walking toward the uprooted house, as if he's abandoned all thought of me. "Climb the hell out and tell me what I'm supposed to do with this wreck." He's talking into the breeze. "I'd say I have a problem here, wouldn't you?"

Arnie Urquhart is changed and changed dramatically from the last time I saw him—at the closing, a decade ago. Every year he's sent me a Christmas card, each one with a shiny color photo showcasing several smiling, healthy-as-all-get-out humans, grouped either on a dense, oak-shaded lawn, grass as green as Augusta, a big, white, rambling red-shuttered house in the background; or the same bunch in cabana attire, tumbled together on the sand, all grins, with a sparkling ocean behind and a golden retriever front and center. I assumed the beach picture to be taken more or less where we are at present, depicting the righteous outcome of things when life goes the way it ought to. At one point a smiling *brown* face became part of the Christmas showcase (female, pretty, young, in some kind of ethnic or tribal costume). Then two years later that face was replaced by an even more broadly smiling blond girl who I thought (for some reason) was Russian. I might've noticed the change in Arnie's looks right then, if I'd been looking closely. But I was never bored enough.

But sometime in the decade Arnie's undergone considerable "work." The Arnie Urquhart I sold my house to—age fifty-four—was a stout, balding, round-belly, thick-knuckled old Wolverine net-minder and only son of a crusty Eastport lobsterman. Arnie had made it off the boat on his hockey skills, then studied history and became a scholar. After graduation, he drove dutifully back to Eastport to be stern-man for his ailing pop, but got "kicked off by the ole man for my own good." After which, he picked up an MBA at Rutgers, worked a decade in institutional provisioning, then went out with his own ideas and made a ton of money running a fancy fish boutique, catering to big-money types in Bernardsville and Basking Ridge. With his Maine-boy solidity, athlete's doggedness, and a lifetime gnosis regarding fish, Arnie (who was a quick read) figured out that what he was selling was authenticity— *his* (as well as Asian Arowana and Golden Osetra). The Schlumberger and Cantor-Fitzgerald bosses all adored him. He showed up personally in the van with his sleeves rolled up, meaty forearms bared, grinning and ready to give great service at a top price. He toted trays, set out canapés, made tireless trips back to the shop, saw to it that every single fishy thing was better than perfect. He reminded his rich customers of the get-your-hands-dirty (and smelly) New England work ethic that made this republic great, powerful, and indomitable and always would, and that they'd gone to Harvard, Yale, and Dartmouth to make sure they never got any closer to than the length of Arnie's sweaty arm.

"I just shake my head, Frank," Arnie said to me, when we were getting the house sold back in '04. "My ole man'd drown each and every one of these cocksuckers like palsied puppies. But I like 'em. They're my bread-and-butter. The moment they're gone—and they *will* be, take my word for it—I'll be right up there in Hopatcong with fish gunk on my hands, delivering lobsters to a whole new limo-full of boy geniuses."

Arnie knew something about the future. How much he knew might've been worth something to somebody paying attention to our economy back in '08.

What's since then happened to Arnie appearance-wise, however, is not much short of alarming. His big face, once scuffed and divoted by a boyhood on the briny, now looks lacquered, as though he'd gone to the islands and picked up some new facial features. There's also something strange about his hair. Arnie, like Corporal Alyss, was never a good-looking brute. And even with whatever strange resurfacings and re-pointings he's gone in for, he's no more handsome than he was, nor any younger-looking—which must've been the goal. He has the same snarly mouth, the same pugnacious chin, the same brick-bat forehead and too-narrow eyes and meaty ears. I'd assumed the new brown face in the Christmas photo had been a son's young wife. But possibly she'd belonged to Arnie, who by then had made some dough and traded up from his original wife—first, for a winsome Shu-Kai, then later on for a busty Svetlana. Along the way he'd felt the need to make the old outer-Arnie keep pace with the spirited, energetic, seemingly ageless inner-essence Arnie. Whatever. His need dictated a Biden-esque transplant to replace his old Johnny-U flattop—a follicle forest that's now grown in but will never look natural. Likewise, the center crevice between Arnie's thick eyebrows has been paved over—the part he formerly utilized to register stare-you-down take-it-or-leave-it's to the high dockside price of halibut and Alaskan crab claws. Plus, the old gulley-gulley of his previously pocked neck now looks the *smoothed* way it did in his '68 Wolverine team picture, when he was known as "Gumper Two" and had the habit of roaring out from between the pipes and kicking your ass if he thought you needed it.

I just have to trust that the old Arnie's in there somewhere. Though, in truth, his re-purposed "look" has left him looking compromised and a little silly and (worst of all) slightly feminized—which couldn't have been what the doctor promised. These decisions are never a good idea.

ARNIE'S WALKED ON AWAY FROM ME AND COME TO stand in front (though also possibly to the side) of our ruined house. He's looking up into what's been skinned open by the wind and water—stark rooms with furniture, plumbing, appliances, ceiling fixtures, white electric harness-work sprung and dangling, giving the shambles a strangely hopeful stage-set look of unfinality, as if something might still be done. It can't. The Democrat-donkey weathervane I nailed to the roof ridge back in '99 at great risk to myself has been bent and busted and left hanging—unrecognizable, if I didn't know what it was and signified. Opposition to "W" Bush.

Arnie's wearing a sharp, brown-leather, thigh-length car coat, high-gloss, low-slung Italian loafers, a pair of cuff-less tweed trousers that probably cost a thousand bucks at Paul Stuart, and a deep-maroon cashmere turtleneck that altogether make him look like a mafia don instead of a high-priced fishmonger.

I've struggled out of my car, tossed my gum, and am instantly cold—my ribs especially—as if I wasn't wearing a shirt under my jacket. The leavening effects of the Gulf Stream are, of course, bullshit. I'm only wearing an old Bean's Newburyport, chinos and deck shoes—at-home attire for the suburban retiree-not-yet-come-fully-to-grips-with-reality. I'm also concerned about stepping on a nail, myself. And because of something Sally said, I feel a need to more consciously pick my feet up when I walk—"the gramps shuffle" being the unmaskable, final-journey approach signal. It'll also keep me from falling down and busting my ass.

What is it about falling? "He died of a fall." "The poor thing never recovered after his fall." "He broke his hip in a fall and was never the same." "Death came relatively quickly after a fall in the back yard." How fucking far do these people fall? Off of buildings? Over spuming cataracts? Down manholes? Is it farther to the ground than it used to be? In years gone by I'd fall on the ice, hop back up, and never think a thought. Now it's a death sentence. What Sally said to me was "Be careful when you go down those front steps, sweetheart. The surface isn't regular, so pick your feet up." Why am I now a walking accident waiting to happen? Why am I more worried about that than whether there's an afterlife?

Fog has pushed in onto the high-tide beach. My cheeks and hands are stinging with damp. The air's hovering at the dew point, ready to turn to water and freeze when the temperature dives. Somewhere nearby a vicious saw whine goes silent. A truck door slams, its engine starts, then revs, then shuts down. The Mexican house gutters, invisible beyond the berm, have knocked off for an early almuerzo. Quiet and wondrous seaside beauty has descended. The ocean's hiss and foghorn are all that's audible.

And like a pilgrim at Agra, I'm struck by my former house's solid stationary-ness, a wreck held in place only by its great weight. It has taken up a persuasive residence on the berm, with its former neighbor houses all gone. It is solemn, still, and slightly mournful teetering so, as if it was aware of its uninhabitability, but determined to re-find dignity in size. I look to my toes to determine if I've got good footing. Something catches my eye, sand crusting over my shoe tops. A bright blue condom lies in front of my toe—out of its wrapper, elongated and spent, its youthful users now far away. I could see it as a gag gift from Poseidon. Though I prefer to see it as a sign that humans are drifting back to this spot already— now that it's vacant—and utilizing the beach as they have and should. Possibly sooner than anyone's predicting, complex life will resume here, and time will march on.

"So. The guy says to me. This putz speculator," Arnie says. We're at a distance from each other. Forces of official-dom have spray-painted a red circle on the broke-open side wall of the house, then divided it into pie-shaped thirds, and inscribed mysterious numbers and letters—code for the struc-ture's present state of body and future. Total loss being the gist of it. Arnie's carrying on talking. It could be to anyone—if anyone else was here. I notice he's lost his old nyak-nyak Maine accent. " . . . he says, this speculator, 'We'll buy your lot, pay to have the derelict hauled off. Write you a check on the spot. 'Cause you're gonna be payin' taxes on the fucker, house or no house. Insurance won't pay. Rates'll be sky high if you *do* rebuild—assuming anybody'll insure you at all. And once the new flood map's issued by fuckin' Obama's lackeys, you'll be sitting on unbuildable ground. If it's not already flooded *again*. Plus the goddamn thing'll have to be up on fucking stilts. Who wants that kind of African rig-up? Beachfront. BFD.'" Arnie shakes his head, staring up at the vacant husk. He sniffs, clears his throat, coughs in the new, approved CDC way—into his elbow. No doubt his new wife has schooled him in this. He would never do it otherwise. "So what's your view, Frank? A disinterested observer? What would *you* do? I said *ix-nay* to three million exactly one year ago. And that was a shit market. I'm fucked, is how you spell it."

"What's the guy offering?" Arnie's a few feet up the berm. I'm not sure I'm being heard.

"Five and change. I told you," Arnie says bitterly. "I was leavin' the place to the kids. My daughter's a diplomat in India. Got her own car and a fuckin' armed driver."

"Do you need the money?" I've come to within a few feet of him, but I'm still talking *up*.

The cotton-y whiteness of the fog has made a cloud of vitreous swimmers swarm my vision, slightly disorienting me. Tiny tadpoles of blood cells, like space junk, shift and subside in my vision—the result of an old Marine Corps cudgel-stick blow to the eye that sent me reeling. They're harmless and would be pretty if they didn't feel like vertigo.

Arnie obviously believes that the money question doesn't require an answer, because he's stuck his hands in his pockets and extended his big chin like Mussolini.

"Was the place paid off, Arnie?" As I said, I haven't consulted my records. I believe cash was exchanged—though a second mortgage is possible.

"Nah," Arnie says. "F-N-C. I paid you cash. You're slip-pin', Frank." He swivels around and looks at me dismissively, a few paces back down the berm from him. There's, of course, a standard calculator for "calamity expense": take the re-build off the value of the house the day *before* disaster struck (October 28th); add twenty-five K as an inconvenience sur-charge, then don't sell the sucker for a farthing less. That, of course, may not work if you can't be certain the ground will be ground and not seawater in ten years. Normally I counsel patience in most things. Patience, though, is a pre-lapsarian concept in a post-lapsarian world.

"If one of these speculators suffered what I've suffered here, you know what would happen to him?" Arnie's turned and started back down the berm, his loafers taking on sand. He's stared at his ruin for long enough. He doesn't really want my advice.

"He'd get richer, Arn," I say.

"So fuck it," Arnie says. "F-U-C-K." Like most con-versations between consenting adults, nothing crucial's been exchanged. Arnie just needed someone to show his mangled house to. And there's no reason that someone shouldn't be me. It's a not-unheard-of human impulse.

Arnie walks right past me in the direction of my car. "You're well out of it, Frank," he says. Close up, I can see better the elements of his new feminized visage. Possibly he forgets how he looks, then remembers and feels skittish and starts looking for an exit. He realizes everyone's seeing the new Arnie, the same way he does in the mirror every morning, and that it's weird as hell. The smoothed-out, previously raveled Gumper forehead, the stupid tree-line hair implantation, the re-paved cheeks and un-ruckled neck. I don't look in mirrors anymore. It's cheaper than surgery.

"Here's what *I'd* do, Arnie," I say to Arnie's back, heading down the berm. "Sell the son of a bitch and let somebody else worry about it. It's OPM. Other people's money." I don't know why, but *I'm* now talking like a Jersey tough guy.

Arnie's not hearing me. He's already down by my car in the shifting fog. It's gotten colder than I want to expose myself to in just my light jacket. My toes are stinging up through my shoe soles.

Arnie stops by my blue car, turns to look at me, where I'm still halfway up the sandy-weedy extrusion, the house shambles behind me. The foghorn emits its baleful call from nowhere. The striper fisherman's long gone. Likewise the Glucks (we always called them the "Clucks"). It's just us. Two men alone, not gay, on an indeterminate mission of consoling and being consoled, which has suddenly revealed itself to be pointless.

Which means trouble could be brewing. Arnie's a man who answers his phone by just saying his name—as though to say, "Yeah? What? Speak your piece or get lost." These men have hair-trigger tempers and can't be trusted to do the right thing. How many *women* answer their phones by saying their names? So much for "I'm here."

"What's this, a fucking Honda? An itchy pussy?" Arnie leans against my car door, as if he's amused by its sky-blue paint job and plastic fenders.

"Hyundai," I say uncomfortably, but take a wrong step on the sandy incline, my toes prickly-numb, my socks damp with sand, my hands clammy. I pitch then half over onto my side, though not all the way onto my face. Not a true fall. "Shit. This fucking sand." I'm balanced like Arnie's house—half on my ass, half on my hand—trying to get my feet under me so I can get off this goddamn sand pillar. I'm afraid of wrenching my neck. Possibly I should roll the rest of the way down.

Arnie's taken no notice. "A hybrid, I suppose." He's still appraising my car. "Like you, Frank." He's all of a sudden supremely satisfied—with something. Dismay and house grief have vanished in the fog. I'm getting myself back on my feet. But has something happened? Is it what I feared—Arnie's turning on me? Possibly he's packing a PPK and will simply shoot me for once selling him a house that's now worth chicken feed. I've let myself in for this. Men are a strange breed.

"A hybrid of what, Arnie," I say with difficulty. "What am I a hybrid of?"

"I'm yanking your schwantz, Frank. You look a little peakèd. You takin' care of yourself?" I'm down off this berm now, my shoes full of cold sand, my ass damp. Arnie, for his part, looks robust, which was what his cosmetic work was in behalf of. He looks to have swelled out his chest a few centimeters and deepened his voice. I don't like being said to be peakèd. "You oughta do yoga, Frank."

I'm back on his level, though unsteady. "I let the machine maintain itself, Arnie."

"Okay," Arnie says. "Probably smart." He's possibly thinking about his cosmetic work in contrast to peakèd me. New grille. New bumpers. In my view, though, Arnie looks like somebody who *used to be* Arnie Urquhart. Age and change have left him squirrelly, and unpredictable—to himself. This is what I witness.

I come to stand beside my Sonata's front headlamp. I'm Christmas cold. Arnie's blocking my path back inside now— unless I want to go around and crawl in the passenger door. I'd like to get in and crank up the heat. But I don't want to seem to want to leave. Arnie—wax-works weirdness and all—is still a man who's lost his house, endured an insult I haven't. He's deserving of a little slack being cut. Our sympathies are most required when they seem least due.

Fog's retreated toward the water's edge, as if the tide change has created a vacuum. A tangy fish stink is all around. I look up through the blue-white mist and can see another Air-Tran jet spiriting upward. I've heard it but haven't registered.

"I need to act quick, I guess," Arnie says, back to his house and the charade that I'm here for real reasons. "That's the way, isn't it?"

"Sometimes," I say, finding the warm hood surface with my hand.

"Fish business is the same. 'Let it sit, you might as well quit. Then you're in the shit.'"

I smile, as if that idea sized up all of life. "It's better than 'hurry up and wait.'"

"That's the old man's mantra." Arnie sniffs, looks down at his own spoiled shoes.

At this small distance of five feet, not looking at him, but letting my eyes roam anywhere but into contact with his, Arnie (in my fervid mind) has magically become not himself, but another boy I also went to Michigan with—Tapper Spitz. I used to bump into Tap in the strangest of places over the years. The Mayo Clinic urology waiting room. The Philadelphia airport cell-phone lot. On the sidewalk outside the My Office bar on Twenty-First and Madison. Tap was likewise a Wolverine puckster. He and Arnie probably knew each other. What did the poet tell us? "All memory resolves itself in gaze." It's much easier at this stressed, empty moment to imagine I'm out here with ole Tapper than that I'm out here with ole Arn. I happen to know Tapman L. Spitz died doing the thing he loved best—para-skiing down the Eiger on his sixty-fifth birthday. RIP ole Tapper.

"My wife doesn't like it down here." Arnie/Tapper snuffles his big, as-yet-unaltered schnoz, then folds his thick arms—not easy in his severely tailored mafia coat. He's staring again up at his house, as if it was where it belonged. I'm supposed to know he means his *new* wife, not the nice, plump-pastie Ishpeming girl I met at the closing, who seemed pleased with life. He shakes his head. "She won't even come down here."

"A reason to cut it loose," I say. Tapper's already sadly fading back where he came from. His service rendered.

"*Oh yeah.*" Arnie's voice is lonely. He's still leaning on my car door, blocking me. A gull has spied us and begun a savage, rhythmical screeching. *Get off the beach, you assholes! It's ours! We want it back. You did your worst. BEAT IT!* "What's the most mysterious thing you know, Frank?" Arnie says, and looks speculative, his lacquered cheeks fattened. He's ready for our conversation to be over, he just doesn't know how to end it—his brain speeding ahead to thoughts of growing his fish business, luring his diplomat daughter home to run things, getting his young wife to take more interest in *his* interests, having things work out better than his make-over makes him feel. His wrecked house, I'm certain, will be gone by New Year's.

"I don't know, Arnie. What universe is our universe inside of? Why do so many people have pancreatic cancer all of a sudden? How does a thermos work? I could come up with several."

Arnie unfolds his crossed arms, pushes his palms back through his hair, both sides, Biden-like, clears his throat, then steps away from my car as if he's realized he was keeping me out of it (my chance now to get out of the chill). Arnie has creases deep as the Clipperton Trench in both his big earlobes. Possibly he feels dark intimations, but wouldn't recognize them.

I inch forward. My neck is already stiffening up after my partial tumble. I've strained something. Arnie's standing back as if he's sold my car to me and is watching me enjoy it for the first time. I'm trying not to be in a rush to get in. Precisely what's happening here between us, I don't really know. A small-scale mystery in itself.

"Did you ever meet Obama, Frank?" Arnie's harsh mouth is raveled by a look of familiar distaste. Why he'd ask this is beyond me.

"Never have, Arnie. No." My hand's on the door handle, squeezing it. "He's not really my kinda guy."

"You voted for him, didn't you?"

"Both times. I think he's great."

"Yeah, yeah. I figured."

My guess is Arnie did, too, but can't admit it.

Over the berm, from where saw and hammering noises have previously floated, the scratchy radio comes on again, at first too loud, then softer. *You're once, twice, three times a la-a-dee* . . . Who sings that? Peabo Bryson? Ludacris? "Eees like, okay, Serena Williams if she was a man," a man's Spanish-spiced voice begins into the cold air over the music. "Se-re-na Williams *eees* a man!" another male voice says back. "Nooo! *Hom-braaay!*" They all crack up. Life's good if you're them.

"You're taller than you used to be, aren't you, Frank?" Arnie's coming toward me now, a smile opening on his strange, half-woman face—as if he knows he's wasted my time but means to make it right before all is lost, the beach returned to the dominion of the gulls, all trace of us gone.

"I have the personality of a shorter man, Arnie." I'm trying to get in my car before Arnie gets closer. I fear an embrace. It could damage my neck and render me an invalid. *Bonding* heads the list of words I've ruled out. Emerson was right—as he was about everything: an infinite remoteness underlies us all. And what's wrong with *that*? Remoteness joins us as much as it separates us, but in a way that's truly mysterious, yet completely adequate for the life ongoing.

Arnie (the idiot) does indeed mean to clap his surprisingly long, leather-cased, net-minder arms around me and pull me—like a puck—into his bosom. A save. I have nowhere to escape to, but try to duck my head as he engulfs me, awfully.

"Enough," I say, my mouth muffled against his goddamn mobster coat, which smells like the inside of his Lexus but also like some epicene men's fragrance Arnie no doubt sprays on, *après le bain,* with his Russian wife keeping stern watch, tapping her toe like Maggie to Jiggs.

"It *is* rough, Franky," Arnie mumbles, wanting me not to feel as bad as I feel about whatever he thinks I feel bad about (being hugged). Clearly he's *here for me* (also on the inventory). A harsh shiver caused by the ocean's chill rattles my ribs—though Arnie may think I've shuddered, possibly even sobbed. Why would I? My house hasn't been ruined. I try to pull away. My back is against the metal door frame so that if I try any harder I'll hurt my neck even more; or worse, fall back in my car with Arnie on top of me, drive the shifter into my C-4 so that the next thing I know the EMS will have me on a board, hauling me back across to Toms River Community, where I've been before and do not ever want to see again. There's nothing I can do—the familiar dilemma for people my age. So what I do—an act of pure desolation—is hug Arnie back, clap my arms around his leathery shoulders and squeeze, as much to save myself from falling. It may not be so different from why anybody hugs anybody. Arnie's hugging me way too hard. My eyes feel bulgy. My neck throbs. The empty space of car seat yawns behind. "Everything could be worse, Frank," Arnie says into my ear, making my head vibrate. He is surely right. Everything could be much worse. Much, much worse than it is.

Everything
Could Be Worse

L AST TUESDAY I READ A PIECE IN THE *NEW York Times* about how it would feel to be tossed out into airless space. This was a small box on a left-hand inside page of the Tuesday Science section, items that rarely venture into the interesting, personal side of things—the stuff a short story by Philip K. Dick or Ray Bradbury would go deeply into with profound (albeit totally irrelevant) moral consequences. These *Times* stories are really just intended to supply lower-rung Schwab execs and apprentice Ernst & Young wage slaves with oddball topics to make themselves appear well-read to their competitor-colleagues during the first warm-up minutes in the office every morning; then possibly to provide the whole day with a theme. ("Careful now, Gosnold, or I'll toss that whole market analysis right out into airless space and you along with it . . ." Eyebrows jinked, smirks all around.)

Nothing's all that surprising about being tossed out into

airless space. Most of us wouldn't stay conscious longer than about fifteen seconds, so that other sensate and attitudinal considerations become fairly irrelevant. The *Times* writer, however, *did* note that the healthiest of us (astronauts, Fijian pearl divers) could actually stay alive and alert for as long as two minutes, unless you hold your breath (I wouldn't), in which case your lungs explode—although, interestingly, not your skin. The data were imprecise about the quality of consciousness that persists—how you might be feeling or what you might be thinking in your last tender moments, the length of time I take to brush my teeth or (sometimes, it seems) to take a leak. It's not hard, though, to imagine yourself mooning around in your bubble hat, trying to come to grips, not wanting to squander your last precious pressurized seconds by giving in to pointless panic. Likely you'd take an interest in whatever's available—the stars, the planets, the green-and-blue wheel of distant Earth, the curious, near-yet-so-far aspect of the mother ship, white and steely, Old Glory painted on the cowling; the allure of the abyss itself. In other words, you'd try to live your last brief interval in a good way not previously anticipated. Though I can also imagine that those two minutes could seem like a mighty long time to be alive. (A great deal of what I read and see on TV anymore, I have to say, seems dedicated to getting me off the human stage as painlessly and expeditiously as possible—making the unknown not be such a bother. Even though the fact that things end is often the most interesting thing about them—inasmuch as most things seem not to end nearly fast enough.)

TEN DAYS BEFORE CHRISTMAS, AS I PULLED INTO MY driveway on Wilson Lane, I saw a woman I didn't know standing on my front stoop. She was facing the door, having possibly just rung the bell and put herself into the poised posture (we've all done it) of someone who has every right to be where she is when a stranger opens the door—and if not *every* right, at least enough not to elicit full-blown hostility.

The woman was black and was wearing a bright red Yuletide winter coat, black, shiny boots, and carried a large black boat of a purse, appropriate to her age—which from the back seemed midfifties. She was also wearing a Christmas-y green-knit tam-o'-shanter pulled down like a cloche, something a young woman wouldn't wear.

I immediately assumed she was a parishioner-solicitor collecting guilt donations for the AME Sunrise Tabernacle over on the still-holding-on black trace of Haddam, beyond the Boro cemetery. In later years, these tidy frame homes have been re-colonized by Nicaraguans and Hondurans who do the gardening, roof repair, and much of the breaking-

and-entering chores out in Haddam Township, or else they run "Mexican" restaurants, where their kids study at poorly lit rear tables, boning up for Stanford and Columbia. These residences have recently faced whacker tax hikes their owners either can't or are too wily to afford. So the houses have become available to a new wave of white young-marrieds who work two jobs, are never home, wouldn't think of having children, and pride themselves on living in a "heritage" neighborhood instead of in a dreary townhouse where everything works but isn't "historic."

A few vestigial Negroes have managed to hold on—by their teeth. Since my wife, Sally, and I moved back to Haddam from The Shore, eight years ago, and into the amply treed President streets—"white housing," roughly the same vintage and stock as the formerly all-black heritage quarter—we've ended up on "lists" identifying us as soft touches for Tanzanian Mission Outreach, or some such worthwhile endeavor. We're likewise the kind of desirable white people who don't show up grinning at *their* church on Sunday, pretending "we belong, since we're all really the same under the skin." Probably we're not.

Snowflakes had begun sifting onto my driveway where I saw the black woman at my door, though a raw sun was trying to shine, and in an hour the sidewalk would have puddles. New Jersey's famous for these not-north/not-south weather

oddities, which render it a never-boring place to live—
hurricanes notwithstanding.

Every week I read for the blind at WHAD, our community station, which was where I was just then driving home from. This fall, I've been reading Naipaul's *The
Enigma of Arrival* (thirty minutes is all they or I can stand),
and in many ways it's a book made for hearing in the dark,
in a chill and tenebrous season. Naipaul, despite apparently
having a drastic and unlikable personality, is as adept as they
get at throwing the gauntlet down and calling bullshit on
the world. From all I know about the blind from the letters
they send me, they're pissed off about the same things he's
pissed off about—the wrong people getting everything, fools
too-long suffered, the wrong ship coming into the wrong
port. Despair misunderstood as serenity. It's also better to
listen to Naipaul and me alone at home than to join some
dismal book club, where the members get drunk on pinot
grigio and go at each other's throats about whether this or
that "anti-hero" reminds them of their ex-husband Herb.
Many listeners say they hear my half hour, then go off to
sleep feeling victorious.

Across the street, my neighbor Mack Bittick still had
his NO SURRENDER ROMNEY-RYAN sign up, though the election's long lost for his side. It sat beside his red-and-white FOR
SALE BY OWNER, which he'd stationed there as if the two signs

meant the same thing. He's an engineer and former Navy SEAL whose job was eliminated by a company in Jamesburg that makes pipeline equipment. He's got big credit card bills and is staring at foreclosure. Mack flies the Stars and Stripes on a pole, day and night, and is one of the brusque-robust, homeschooling, canned-goods-stock-piling, non-tipper, free-market types who're averse to paying commissions on anything ("It's a goddamn *tax* on what we oughta get for fuckin' free by natural right . . .") and don't like immigrants. He's also a personhood nutcase who wants the unborn to have a vote, hold driver's licenses, and own handguns so they can rise up and protect him from the revolution when it comes. He's always eager to pick my old-realtor brain, sounding me out about trends and price strategies, and ways to bump up his curb appeal on the cheap, so he can maximize equity and still pocket his homestead exemption. I do my utmost to pass along the worst possible realty advice: never *ever* negotiate; demand your price or fuck it; don't waste a nickel on superficial niceties (your house should look "lived in"); don't act friendly to potential buyers (they'll grow distrustful); leave your Tea-Party reading material and gun paraphernalia out on the coffee table (most home buyers already agree with you). He, of course, knows I voted for Obama, who he feels should be in prison.

WHEN THE RED-COATED BLACK WOMAN AT MY FRONT door realized no one was answering, and that a car had crunched into the snowy driveway, she turned and issued a big welcoming smile down to whoever was arriving, and a demure wave to assure me all was well here—no one hiding in the bushes with burglar tools, about to put a padded brick through my back window. Black people bear a heavy burden trying to be normal. It's no wonder they hate us. I'd hate us, too. I was sure Mack Bittick was watching her through the curtains.

For a moment I thought the woman might be Parlance Parker—grown-up daughter of my long-ago housekeeper, Pauline, from the days when I lived on Hoving Road, on Haddam's west side, was married to my first wife, our children were little, and I was trying unsuccessfully to write a novel. Pauline ran our big Tudor house like a boot camp—mustering the children, working around Ann, berating me for not having a job, and sitting smoking on our back steps like a drill sergeant. Like me, she hailed from Mississippi and, because we were both now "up north," could treat me with disdain, since I'd renounced all privileges to treat her like a subhuman. Pauline died of a brain tumor thirty years ago. But her daughter Parlance recognized me one Saturday morning in the Shop 'n Save and threw her arms around me like a lost relation. Since then she's twice shown up at the door, wanting to "close the circle," tell me how much her mother loved us all, hear stories about the children (whom she never knew), and generally re-affiliate with a lost part of life over which she believes I hold dominion.

I got out of my car, advertising my own welcoming "I know you're probably not robbing me" smile. The woman was not Parlance. Something told me she was also not one of the AME Sunrise Tabernacle ladies either. But she was someone. That, I could see.

"Hi!" I sang out in my most amiable, Christmas-cheer voice. "You're probably looking for Sally." There was no reason to believe that. It was just the most natural-sounding thing I could think to say. Sally was actually in South Mantoloking, counseling grieving hurricane victims—something she's been doing for weeks.

The woman came down onto the walk, still smiling. I was already cold, dressed only in cords, a double-knit polo, and a barracuda jacket—dressed for the blind, not for the winter.

"I'm Charlotte Pines, Mr. Bascombe," the woman said, smiling brightly. "We don't know each other."

"Great," I said, crossing my lawn, snow sifting flake by flake. The still-green grass had a meringue on top that had begun to melt. Temps were hovering above freezing.

Ms. Pines was medium sized but substantial, with a shiny, kewpie-doll pretty face and skin of such lustrous, variegated browns, blacks, and maroons that any man or woman would've wished they were black for at least part of every day. She was, anyone could see, well-to-do. Her red coat with a black fur collar I picked out as cashmere. Her black boots hadn't come cheap either. When I came closer, still stupidly grinning, she took off one leather glove, extended her hand, took mine in a surprisingly rough grip, and gave it a firm I'm-in-charge squeezing. I felt like a schoolboy who meets his principal in Walmart and shakes hands with an adult for the first time.

"I'm making a terrible intrusion on you, Mr. Bascombe."

"It's fine," I said. "I like intrusions." For some reason I was breathless. "I was just reading for the blind. Sally's over in Mantoloking." I had the Naipaul under my arm. Ms. Pines was a lady in her waning fifties. Snow was settling into the wide part of her beauty-parlor hair, the third not covered by her tam. She'd spoken very explicitly. Conceivably she had moments before gotten out of a sleek, liveried Lincoln now waiting discreetly down the block. I took a quick look down Wilson but saw nothing. I saw what I believed was a flicker in the Bitticks' front curtains. Black people don't visit in our neighborhood that often, except to read the meter or fix something. However, that Ms. Pines had simply *appeared* conferred upon me an intense feeling of well-being, as if she'd done me an unexpected favor.

"I haven't met your wife," Ms. Pines said. Somewhere back in the distant days she'd been a considerable and curvaceous handful. Even in her Barneys red coat, that was plain. She'd now evolved into dignified, imposing pan-African handsomeness.

"She's great," I said.

"I'm certain," Ms. Pines said and then was on to her business. "I'm on a strange mission, Mr. Bascombe." Ms. Pines seemed to rise to a more forthright set-of-shoulders, as if an expected moment had now arrived.

"Tell me," I said. I nearly said *I'm all ears,* words I'd never said in my life.

"I grew up in your house, Mr. Bascombe." Ms. Pines' shoulders were firmly set. But then unexpectedly she seemed to lose spirit. She smiled, but a different smile, a smile summoning supplication and regret, as if she *was* one of the AME ladies, and I'd just uttered something slighting. She swiveled her head around and regarded the front door, as if it had finally opened to her ring. She had a short but still lustrous neck that made her operate her shoulders a bit stiffly. Everything about her had suddenly altered. "Of course it looks very different now." She was going on trying to sound pleasant. "This was back in the sixties. It seems much smaller to me." Her smile brightened, as she found me again. "It's nicer. You've kept it nice."

"Well, that's great, too," I said. I'd proclaimed greatness three times now, even though sentimental returns of the sort Ms. Pines was making could never be truly great. "Mightily affecting." "Ambiguously affirming." "Bittersweet and troubling." "Heart-wrenching and sad." All possible. But probably not great.

Only, I wanted her to know none of it was bad news. Not to me. It was *good* news, in that it gave us—the two of us, cold here together—a *great* new connection that didn't need to go further than my front yard, but might. This was how things were always supposed to work out.

Previous-resident returns of this sort, in fact, happen all the time and have happened to me more than once. Possibly in nineteenth-century Haddam they didn't. But in twenty-first-century Haddam they do—where people sell and buy houses like Jeep Cherokees, and where boom follows bust so relentlessly realtors often leave the FOR SALE sign in the garage; and where you're likely to drive to the Rite Aid for a bottle of Maalox and come home with earnest money put down on that Dutch Colonial you'd had your eye on and just happened to see your friend Bert the realtor stepping out the front door with the listing papers in hand. No one wants to stay any place. There are species-level changes afoot. The place you used to live and brought your bride home to, taught your kid to ride his bike in the driveway, where your old mother came to live after your father died, then died herself, and where you first noticed the peculiar tingling movement in your left hand when you held the *New York Review* up near the light—*that* place may now just be two houses away from where you *currently* live (but wished you didn't), though you never much think about having lived there, until one day you decide to have a look.

At least four prior owner/occupants have come to visit houses I've lived in over these years. I've always thrown the doors open, once it was clear they weren't selling me burial insurance and I'd gotten my wallet off the hall table. I've just stood by like a docent and let them wander the rooms, grunting at this or that update, where a wall used to be, or recalling how the old bathroom smelled on Sunday mornings before church. On like that, until they can get it all straight in their minds and are ready to go. Usually it takes no longer than ten minutes—standard elapsed time for re-certifying sixty years of breathing existence. Generally it's the over-fifties who show up. If you're much younger, you've got it all recorded on your smartphone. And it's little enough to do for other humans— help them get their narrative straight. It's what we all long for, unless I'm mistaken.

"I don't suppose, Mr. Bascombe . . ." Ms. Pines was taking another anxious peek around at my house, then back to me, smiling in her new defeated way. " . . . I don't suppose I could step in the front door and have one quick look inside." Kernels of dry snow were settling onto her cheeks, her coat shoulders and the onyx uppers of her boots. My hair had probably gone white. We were a fine couple. Though right at that second I experienced a sudden, ghostly whoosh of vertigo—something I've been being treated for, either along with or because of C-3 neck woes. The world's azimuth just suddenly goes catty-wampus—and I could end up on my back. Though it can also, if I'm sitting down, be half agreeable—like a happy, late-summer, Saturday-evening zizz, when you've had a tumbler of cold Stoli and the Yanks are on TV. In my bed table I have pages of corrective exercise diagrams to redress these episodes. My "attack" on the lawn just whooshed in and whooshed out, like a bat flitting past a window at dusk. One knows these moments, of course, to be warnings.

"Okay. Sure. You bet you can," I almost shouted this, trying to make myself not seem demented. Ms. Pines looked at me uncertainly, possibly stifling the urge to ask, "Are you okay?" (No more grievous words can be spoken in the modern world.) "Come with me," I said, still too loud, and grappled her plump arm the way an octogenarian would. We lurched off toward my stoop steps, which were snow covered and perilous. "Watch your step here," I said, as much to myself as to her.

"This is very kind of you," Ms. Pines said almost inaudibly, coming along in my grip. "I hope it's not an inconvenience . . ."

"It's *not* an inconvenience," I said. "It's nothing at all. Su casa es mi casa . . ." I said the reverse of what I meant. It's not that unusual anymore.

THE BIG LG, WHICH I'D LEFT ON IN THE LIVING room when I'd gone for my blind-reading, was in full ESPN cry when I opened the front door, the sound jacked way up. On the screen a beefy, barrel-shaped man in camo gear—face smudged with self-eliminating paint, and seated in a camo'd wheelchair—was just at that moment squeezing off, from an enormously-scoped, lethally-short-barreled black rifle propped on some kind of dousing stick, a terrible bullet aimed in the direction of a gigantic bull elk, possibly two thousand yards away across a pristine, echoing Valhalla-like mountainscape.

BOOM!

The entire mountain—plus my living room and the vaulted sky above it—quaked, then went deaf at the awful sound.

BOOM! Again the terrible report. The sun went dark,

avalanches broke free, tiny sylvan creatures beside faraway alpine rills looked guardedly toward the heavens.

The elk—grazing, calm, thinking who-knows-what elk thoughts—suddenly went all weird and knee-wiggly, as if its parts had simultaneously resigned their roles. After which, in exactly one second, its head rose slightly as though it had heard something (it had), then it went right over like a candlepin into the dust-burst the bullet had kicked up, having passed straight through the creature as if it was butter.

"Wooo-hooo-hooo-hooo! Woooooo!" a man's voice somewhere out of the picture began woo-hooing. "Ooooh *man,* oh man, oh man!"

"I *am* a deadly motherfucker," the wheelchair marksman said (I could read his lips), his rifle across his unfeeling knees. He turned toward whoever was woo-hooing, a great crazed smile on his fat camo face. "It doesn't get any better than this, does it, Arlo? *Does* it? Oh sweet Jesus . . ."

I quick ditched the Naipaul onto the couch, got my hands on the clicker, and doused the picture. I'd earlier been watching the NFL injury rundown, hoping to see if the Giants had a snowball's chance against the Falcons on Sunday. They didn't.

My house's interior, absent the ear-warping TV clamor, became, then, intergalactically silent. And still. Like a room a security camera was guarding—a secret view for a stranger's secret purposes. I often imagine myself as "a figure" in an elevator, being viewed through the grainy lens of just such a secreted camera. Mute. Unmindful. Generic—waiting for my floor, then the door opening, and (in my imagining) a hooded man stepping in before I can step out, and beginning to berate me or pummel me or shoot me at close range. (I watch too much television.) The head shrinkers at Mayo—where I get my prostate re-checks—would have a field day with my data set. There's a side to this little drama that doesn't make me look good, I realize—not someone you'd trust to run a day care or even a dog rescue.

Though shouldn't our complex mental picture of ourselves at least partly include such a neutralized view? Not just the image that smiles wryly back from the shaving mirror; but the solitary trudger glimpsed in the shop window, shoulders slumped, hairline backing away, neck flesh lapping, bent as if by winds—shuffling down the street to buy the *USA Today*? Is that person not worth keeping in mind and paid a modicum? If not a round of huzzahs, at least a tip of the hat? A high five (or at least a low one)? I don't share every view with Sally, who'd shout the rafters down with laughter if she knew *all* my innermost thoughts.

"My goodness," Ms. Pines said from behind me, inside the tiny foyer now—my silent house's primordial self suddenly all around her in a way anyone would find startling. It's too bad we don't let ourselves in for more unexpected moments. Life would be less flimsy, feel more worth preserving. The suburbs are supposedly where nothing happens, like Auden said about what poetry doesn't do; an over-inhabited faux terrain dozing in inertia, occasionally disrupted by "a Columbine" or "an Oklahoma City" or a hurricane to remind us what's really real. Though plenty happens in the suburbs—in the way that putting a drop of water under an electron microscope reveals civilizations with histories, destinies, and an overpowering experience of the present. "Well. Yes. My goodness, my goodness," Ms. Pines kept saying in the front entry, the storm door sucking closed behind her, letting outside snow light in around her. "I don't quite know what to say." She was shaking her kewpie-doll head that either so much had changed or so little had. We've kept the "older-home" fussiness of small rooms, one-way-to-get-anywhere, an inset plaster phone nook, upstairs transoms, and all original fixtures except the kitchen. Sally hates the spiritless open-concept bleakness of the re-purposed. *Do I really need a fucking greenhouse?* is the way she put it.

"I don't want to track in snow," Ms. Pines said.

"The maid'll clean it up," I said. A joke.

"Okay," she said, in wonderment still. "I . . ."

"How long since you were here?" I said, still in the TV-silent living room. Ms. P., in the foyer, inched toward the foot of the stairs. The narrow hallway past the basement door and on to the kitchen lay ahead—the same house is on thousands of streets, Muncie to Minot.

Her gaze for a moment carried up the stairs, her lips a tiny bit left apart. "I'm sorry?" she said. She'd heard me but didn't understand.

"Have you visited before? Since you lived here?"

"Oh. No," Ms. Pines said, registering. "Never. I walked out of this house—this door . . ." She turned toward the glass storm door behind her. " . . . in nineteen sixty-nine, when I was almost seventeen. I was a junior. At Haddam High. I walked to school."

"My kids went there," I said.

"I'm sure." She looked at me strangely then, as if my presence was a surprise. From the warmth of her red coat, enforced by the warmth of my house, Ms. Pines had begun exuding a sweet floral aroma. *Old Rose.* A fragrance some-one older might've worn. Possibly her mother had sniftered it on upstairs in front of the medicine-cabinet mirror, before an evening out with her husband. Where, I wondered, did Negroes go for fun in Haddam, pre-1969? Trenton?

"You're absolutely welcome to look around," I said, extra-obligingly.

"Oh, that's very kind, Mr. Bascombe. I'm feeling a little light-headed." She re-righted her shoulders and took a firmer grip on her big patent-leather purse. Snow had puddled on the area rug inside the doorway. She was transfixed.

"Let me get you a glass of orange juice," I said, stepping off past her and down the hall toward the kitchen, where it smelled of Sally's morning bacon and the Krups cooking breakfast coffee to licorice. I hauled out the Minute Maid carton, found a plastic glass, gushed it full, and came back as fast as I could. Why OJ seemed the proper antidote to being transfixed is anybody's guess.

"That's very nice. Thank you so much," Ms. Pines said. She hadn't budged. I put the glass into her un-gloved hand. She took a dainty sip, swallowed, cleared her throat softly, and smiled, touching her glove to her lips, then handed me back the glass, which had decals of leaping green porpoises, from our years on The Shore—gone now except for the glasses. The old-rose fragrance was dense around Ms. Pines, mingling with a faint tang of intimate perspiration.

"Let me take your coat."

"Oh, no," Ms. Pines said. "I'm not going to impose any-more."

From the basement, the heat pump came smoothly to life. A distant murmur.

"You should just look around," I said. "I don't have to go with you. I'll sit in the kitchen and read the paper or refill the bird feeder for the squirrels. I'm retired. I'm just waiting to die, or for my wife to come back from Mantoloking—whichever's first."

"Well," Ms. Pines said, smiling fraily, letting her eyes follow up the stairs. "That's very generous. If you really don't mind, I'll just look upstairs at my old room. Or *your* room." She blinked at the prospect, then looked at me.

"Great!" I said for the fourth time. "Take your good sweet time. You know where the kitchen is. You won't find things much changed."

"Well," Ms. Pines said. "We'll have to see."

"That's why you're here," I said and went off down the hall to leave her to it.

FOR A TIME, I HEARD MS. PINES—MOUNTING THE stairs, the risers squeezing, the floor joists muttering as she stepped room to room. She emitted no personal sounds I could hear via the registers or the stairwell. I'd already read the *Times*. So, I sat contentedly at the breakfast table, meager snowfall cluttering the back-yard air, caking on the rhododendrons and the Green Egg smoker. On a legal pad, I'd begun jotting down some entries for the monthly feature I write for the *We Salute You* magazine, which we hand out free of charge in airports to our troops returning home from Iraq and Afghanistan, or wherever our country's waging secret

wars and committing global wrongs in freedom's name—
Syria, New Zealand, France. *We Salute You* contains helpful
stateside info and easy how-to's—in case a vet's memory's
been erased—along with phone numbers and addresses and
contact data that the troopers, swabbies, airmen, and marines
might need during their first critical hours back in the world.

My column's called "WHAT MAKES *THAT* NEWS?"
It contains oddball items I glean out of "the media" that don't
really approximate fresh thought—that in fact often violate
the concept of thought by being plug-obvious, asinine, or
both—but that still come across our breakfast tables every
morning or flashed through our smartphones (I don't own
one) *disguised* as news. Veterans often come back after a year
of dodging bullets, seeing their pals' limbs blown off, endur-
ing unendurable heat, eating sand, and learning to trust no
one—even the people they want to trust—with a fairly well-
established sense that no one back home, the people they're
fighting, dying, and wasting their lives *for,* knows dick about
anything that really matters, and might just as well go back to
the third grade or be shot to death drive-by style (which is why
so many of our troops are eager to re-up). My column tries to
take a bit of the edge off by letting soldiers know we're not *all*
as dumbass as newts back home, and in fact some of the idiotic stuff in the news can be actually hilarious, so that suicide
can be postponed to a later date.

One item I'm including for January is a study up at Harvard that found a direct correlation between chronic pain and loss of sleep. If you hurt twenty-four hours a day, sleep's hard to come by—the Harvard scientists detected. WHAT MAKES *THAT* NEWS? These things aren't difficult to find.

In November, I included one from a top-notch sports medicine think tank in Fort Collins, where kinesiologists noticed that running slowly and not very far was much better for you, over a ten-year period, than running forty minutes or farther than eight miles—which, it turns out, *increases* the likelihood you'll die sooner rather than later. WHAT MAKES *THAT* NEWS?

And one I'd seen just the day before, and was noting at the breakfast table, was out of the *Lancet* in the UK and represented a conclusion drawn at the Duchess of Kent Clinic in Shropshire (the same person who hands over the Wimbledon trophy, though she always seems like someone who couldn't care less about tennis or even understand it). The doctors in Shropshire noticed that in cases of repetitive thought patterning leading to psychic decline, lengthy institutionalization, and eventually suicide, the most common cause-agent seemed to be not trying hard enough to think about something pleasant. WHAT MAKES *THAT* NEWS?

My pen name—it seemed appropriate—is "HLM."

The magazine often forwards me letters from vets who say that these squibs—which I include without comment—have brightened their first hours back and taken their minds off what most anybody's mind would likely run to, if twenty-four hours before you'd been pinned down by enemy fire in Waziristan, but now find yourself in the Department of Motor Vehicles, trying to get your driver's license renewed, and are being told by a non–English speaker that you don't have the six pieces of ID necessary, plus a major credit card with your name spelled exactly like your passport.

Mayhem. That's what you'd be thinking hard about. And no one would blame you. Statistics, however, show that great cravings of almost any nature, including a wish to assassinate, can be overcome just by brief interludes of postponement—the very thing no one ever believes will work, but does. That *IS* news.

Ms. Pines had been up above for almost five minutes. I heard her begin stepping heavily, carefully down the stairs—as if she were descending sideways. "Umm-hmmm, umm-hmmm." I heard her make this noise, one "umm-hmmm" per step, as if she was digesting something she'd just taken in. I swiveled around in my chair so I could see to the front door, wanting her to feel at home and recognized when she came back into view. Maybe she'd want to sit down in the living room and watch *The Price Is Right* while I finished up some chores. Later, I'd heat up last night's lasagna, and we'd get to know each other in new and consequential ways.

Ms. Pines—small, red-coated figure, boatish purse, green tam, shiny boots—appeared at the bottom of the stairs. She did start to walk into the living room, then realized the hall was beside her and that "a presence" (me) was twenty feet away—watching her. "Oh," she said and flashed her big, relieved, but also embarrassed smile. She set her shoulders as she'd done before. "I guess I entered a dream state for a while up there," she said. "It's silly. I'm sorry."

"It's *not* silly," I said, arm bent over the chair back *Our Town* style—our conversation being carried down the short hallway as if we were communicating out of separate life realms, which possibly we were. "It's too bad more people don't do what you're doing," I said. "The world might be a better place." Almost all conversations between myself and African Americans devolve into this phony, race-neutral natter about making the world a better place, which we assume we're doing just by being alive. But it's idiotic to think the world would be a better place if more people barged uninvited into strangers' homes. I needed, though, to say *something,* and wanted it to be optimistic and wholesome and seem to carry substance—even if it didn't.

"Well," Ms. Pines said. "I don't know." She'd recovered, but didn't appear to know what to do. She wasn't tacking toward the front door, but wasn't advancing toward me in the breakfast room/sunporch either. Poise had given way to perplexity. "Is that still the door to the cellar?" She was eyeing the basement door halfway down the shadowed hall between us. Her eyes seemed to fix on the glass knob, then switched up to me, as if the door might burst open and reveal who knew what.

"It is," I said over my chair back. "It's full of spooks down there." Not ideal.

Ms. Pines pursed her lips, exhaled an audible breath. "I'm sure."

"Want to take a gander?" Another phrase I'd never uttered in my life on earth—but wary not to say something to make the world an even less good place: "It's black as coal down there . . . dingy as hell, too . . . venture down there, and the jig'll be up." Words were failing me more than usual. Better to use fewer of them.

"There's probably some places one oughtn't go," Ms. Pines said.

"I feel that way about California," I said over the chair back. "Colorado, too. And Texas."

Ms. Pines cast a patient-impatient smile toward me. She

seemed about to say something, then didn't. And by refrain-
ing, she immediately took command not just of me and our
moment, but somehow of my entire house. I didn't really
mind.

"How did your family come to live here?" I said. Would
I ask a white person that? ("Dad moved us all out here from
Peoria in '58, and we had a heckuva time at first . . .") For
most questions there's an answer.

"Oh, well," Ms. Pines said from the foyer, "my father
grew *up* in Haddam. On Clio Street." She ventured a step
nearer into the hall. "That's the muse of history."

"Come sit down," I said and popped up, pushing a second wire-back café chair—Sally's—away from the table for
her to occupy.

She came toward me, looking left, then right, assessing
what we'd done to the hall and the kitchen and the breakfast sunroom. New therma-panes where there'd been gunked
patio doors. Green, replica Mexican tiles. A prior owner had
"opened out the kitchen" twenty years ago, then moved away
to Bernardsville.

"It's all very nice," Ms. Pines said, looking over-dressed
now in her red Christmas coat and mistletoe topper. Her
presence was like having a census taker visit and surprisingly
become your friend.

"I've got some coffee made."

Ms. Pines was still looking around the sunroom, her eyes stopping on my cherished, framed Block Island map. "Where's that?" she said, furrowing a brow, as if the map was a problem.

"Block Island," I said. "I went there years ago. It's in Rhode Island, which most people don't know." Bzzz, bzzz, bzzz.

"I see." She set her big purse on the floor and seated herself primly in the café chair.

"Take off your coat," I said. "It's warm." Sally, lifetime Chicagoan, is always cold.

"Thank you." She unbuttoned her red coat to reveal a green, wool two-piece suit sporting good-sized gold buttons and a Peter Pan collar. Pricey but stylish, and right for a woman of her vintage. With her coat off, her left arm also revealed the blunt end of a cumbersome white-plaster cast above her black gloved hand. "I have this wound to contend with." She frowned at the cast's bulk.

"How'd you manage that?" I set a yellow mug of coffee down, the sugar bowl, milk caddy, and a spoon. Old Rose was in the air again, not all that agreeable with the coffee aroma. She removed her other glove and laid it on the table.

"I'm a hurricane victim," she said, arranging both her hands, cast and all, on the glass table surface. She said *hurricane* to sound like "hair-a-cun," then inhaled a considerable breath, which she let out slowly. I all at once sensed I *was* about to hear an appeal for the Mount Pisgah cemetery maintenance fund, or some Nationalist Chinese outreach. "My home is in Lavallette," Ms. Pines said. "We took a pretty considerable beating. I'm lucky I only broke my arm."

"I'm sorry you did," I said brightly, wrong about the solicitation. "Is your house intact?"

"It was ruined." Ms. Pines smiled ruefully at her coffee, deliberately spooning in sugar. "I had a nice condominium." She made the same "umm-hmmm" sound she'd made on the stairs. The sugar spoon tinkled as she moved it.

No words came out of me. Words can also be the feeblest emissaries for our feelings. Ms. Pines seemed to understand what silence signified.

"I'm back over here because of that," she said, and lifted her chin as she stirred her coffee, then regarded me in what looked like an unexpected sternness. "I have friends in Haddam. On Gulick Road. They're putting me up until I can determine what to do."

"I'm sure you had insurance," I said, my second, or possibly third, idiotic remark in five minutes.

"Everyone had insurance." Ms. Pines right-handedly brought her coffee to her lips. I'd forgotten a napkin and jumped up, snatched a paper one out of the kitchen holder, and set it beside her spoon. "We just don't know," she said, setting her mug onto the napkin. "Haddam CC 4-Ball" was printed on it—a memento of my former wife, Ann, from long, long ago.

"Do you have a family?" I said.

"I had a husband," Ms. Pines said. "We separated in '01. He passed on in '04. I kept our apartment. He was a police sergeant."

"I see." *I'm deeply sorry* wouldn't have worked any better than *Oh, great, that's perfect. He's out of the way. And you're still damn good looking.* Words.

"I teach high school in Wall Township," Ms. Pines said, dabbing her lips. "We shut school down after the storm. Which isn't the worst thing that could happen to me under these circumstances." She regarded her busted-arm cast. "Our students are in limbo, of course. We'll have to make provisions for them after Christmas." She smiled at me with grim Christmas-no-cheer and took another sip of coffee.

"What do you teach?" I said, across the table. Snow had ceased in my small back yard, leaving the air mealy gray. A pair of enormous, self-important crows had arrived to scrounge in the pachysandra below the suet feeder.

"History," Ms. Pines said. "I'm a Barnard grad. From '76. The bicentennial year."

"That's great," I said. "My daughter almost went there."

Another silence invoked itself. I could've told her I'd

gone to Michigan, have two children, an ex-wife and a current one, that I'd sold real estate here and at The Shore for twenty years, once wrote a book, served in an undistinguished fashion in the marines, and was born in Mississippi—bangety, bangety, bangety, boop. Or I could let silence do its sovereign work, and see if something of more material import opened up. It would be a loss if some hopeful topic couldn't now be broached, given all. Nothing intimate, sensitive, or soul-baring. Nothing about the world becoming a better place. But something any two citizens could talk about, any ole time, to mutual profit—our perplexing races notwithstanding.

"You said your father grew up here?" I smiled what must've been a loony smile, but a signal of where our conversation might veer if we let it.

"He did. Yes," Ms. Pines said and cleared her throat formally. "He was the first of his family to attend college. He played football at Rutgers. In the '50s. He did extremely well. Studied engineering. Took his doctorate. He became the first Negro to work at a high level at Bell Laboratories. He was an audio specialist. He was very smart."

"Like Paul Robeson," I blurted—in spite of every living cell urging me not to say "Like Paul Robeson."

"Um-hm," Ms. Pines said, uninterested in Paul Robeson. "Some people are better as ideas than as humans, Mr. Bascombe. My father was that sort of man. I think he thought of himself as an idea more than as a man. Our race suffers from that."

"So does ours," I said, glad to see Paul Robeson drift off downstream.

"We lived in this house," Ms. Pines said, "from 1959 to 1969. My father insisted on living in a white neighborhood. Though it didn't work out very well."

"Did your mother not like it?" Why would I assume that?

"Yes. My mother was an opera singer. Or would've been. She was out of place wherever she was. She was Italian. She preferred New York—where she was from. I was the only one of us who truly liked it in Haddam. I loved going to school. My brother didn't have an easy time."

"I'm sorry," I said.

"Well." Ms. Pines looked away out the sliding door, where the crows were standing atop the melting snow-crust gawking in at us through the window. "I considered calling you before I came."

"Why?" I said, smiley, smiley, smiley.

"I was nervous. Because if you knew who I was—or am—possibly you wouldn't have liked me to come."

"Why?" I said. "I'm glad you came."

"Well. That's kind."

"They sound like interesting people. I'm sorry I didn't know them. Your parents."

"Do you *not* know about them?" Ms. Pines eyed me appraisingly, her chin raised a guarded inch. She placed her un-injured hand on top of the one that had the cast and breathed audibly. "Hartwick Pines?" she intoned. "You don't know about him?"

"No," I said. "Was that his name?" A name reminiscent of a woodwinds camp in the Michigan forests. Or a Nuremberg judge. Or a signatory of Dumbarton Oaks.

"I'd have thought they were infamous."

"What did they do?" I said.

"And you don't know?" Ms. Pines said.

"Tell me."

"I really didn't mean to venture into this, Mr. Bascombe. I only felt required to *come*—after living not very far away for so long a time. I'm sorry."

"I'm really glad you did," I said. "I try to visit all the places I've lived at least once every ten years. It puts things in perspective. Everything's smaller—like *you* said."

"I imagine," Ms. Pines said. As expected, we'd banged right into something with meat on its bones: being the first Negroes in a white suburban neighborhood with a boy-genius father and a high-strung temperamental operatic white mother. It had the precise mix of history and mystery the suburbs rarely get credit for—a story *60 Minutes* or *The NewsHour* could run with; or ESPN, if the old man had been a standout for the Crimson Knights, gotten drafted by the Giants but chose the life of the mind instead. Even better if the mother had made it at least into the chorus at the Met, and the brother became a priest or a poet. There was even a possible as-told-to angle I could write. People tell me things. I also listen, and have a pleasant, absorptive, non-judgmental face, which made me a good living in the realty business (though doesn't make me anything these days).

"Do you ever dream about yourself when you were young, Mr. Bascombe?" Ms. Pines said, blinking at me. "Not that you're old, of course."

"Frank," I said. "Yes, I do. I'm always twenty-eight in my dreams, and I have a mustache and smoke a pipe. I actually try not to remember my dreams. Forgetting's better."

"I'm sure you're right," Ms. Pines said, staring at the yellow rim of her Haddam CC 4-Ball mug.

Just at that precise instant one of the cloudy little gut bubbles we all experience descended distressingly out of my stomach and down, in such a blazing hurry-up, I barely caught it and clamped the exit shut. One more second would've cast a bad atmosphere on everything and everyone. My son Paul Bascombe used to call this being "fartational." Memps, our oncologist-neighbor's wiggly, old red wiener dog from our days on Cleveland Lane, was forever wandering nosily into our house and cutting big stinkers, one after another. "Out! Memps," Paul would loudly decree (with relish). "Memps is fartational! Out, bad Memps!" Poor Memps would scuttle out the door, as if he knew—though not without a couple more salvos.

I was disconcertingly "all-but-Memps"—though not detectably, thanks be to god. It must've shown, though, in my mouth's rigorous set, because Ms. Pines' sloe eyes rose to me, settled back to her coffee mug rim, then fastened on me again as if I might be "experiencing" something, another episode, like my vertigo whoosh twenty minutes ago that I thought she hadn't seen, but that might require a 911 call this time around—like her husband. Lentil soup was the culprit.

"I feel like I'll be dying at the right time," I said—why, I didn't know—as though that had been the thread we'd been following; *not* whether our dreams were worth remembering; or what it was like to be a Negro in apartheid Haddam and have high-strung, overachieving parents for whom nothing could be normal. A squiggle of lower bowel pain made me squirm, then went its way.

"Are you dying now?" Ms. Pines looked concerned, and impatient—in case I was.

"I don't think so," I said. "I was thinking yesterday about all the animal species that were on the planet when I was born and that are still around. Pretty soon they won't be. It's probably a good time to be checking out."

Ms. Pines seemed puzzled. Who wouldn't be? We'd been on the brink of a revelation. Possibly dramatic. Clearly she wanted to get back to it. She was operating on strong imperative now. Unlike me. "I . . ." she started to say, then stopped and shook her head, on which was perched her Christmas tam, which she'd forgotten about and that made her look ever-so-slightly elfin, but still dignified.

"I have dream conversations with my son Ralph," I said. "He died in '79. He's forty-three in my dreams and a stockbroker. He gives me investment advice. I enjoy thinking it could be true."

Ms. Pines just began, without responding. "My father, when we lived here, Mr. Bascombe, became distrustful. And very insular. He'd advanced at Bell by honest effort and genius. But it didn't, somehow, make him very happy. His parents lived over a few blocks on Clio. But we never saw *them*. He hardly ever went out in his yard. Which made my mother more restless and unhappy than she already was. She believed she belonged onstage at the Metropolitan, and marrying my father had been a serious miscalculation. Though I believe she loved him. She had my brother, Ellis, and me to bring up, though. So she was trapped here."

"That doesn't sound good," I said. Though it didn't sound like anything white people on every block in Haddam didn't have a patent on. We're always environed by ourselves.

"Well," Ms. Pines said. "Ellis and I didn't know how bad it had become. We were quite happy children. Ellis didn't prosper in school, but had a lovely singing voice, which made our mother dote on him. I did *very* well in school, which pleased my *father*. In that way it wasn't so unusual for any American family."

"I was thinking that," I said. "Sounds like a story in *The New Yorker*."

Ms. Pines looked at me with incomprehension. I was suddenly one of the in-limbo underachievers in Wall Township, who'd just made an inappropriate joke about the Compromise of 1850 and needed to be ignored.

"I'm not sure you need to hear this, Mr. Bascombe," Ms. Pines said. "I don't require to tell it. I'm happy just to leave. You've been more than kind. It's not a happy story."

"You're alive to tell it," I said. "You survived. Whatever doesn't kill us makes us stronger, right?" I don't, of course, believe this. Most things that don't kill us right off, kill us later.

"I've wanted to believe that," Ms. Pines said. "It's the history teacher's bedrock. The preparation for bad times."

History's just somebody else's *War and Peace,* is what I thought. Though there was no reason to argue it. I smiled at her encouragingly.

Diaphanous mist rose off the scabby snow outside the

window, making my yard look derelict and un-pretty. The house gave a creaking noise of age and settlement. A spear of pure, rarefied mid-December sunlight illuminated a square on the hickory trunk in the neighbors' yard across the bamboo fence behind the potting shed the hurricane had damaged— the D'Urbervilles, a joint-practice lawyer couple. It could've been April, with balmy summer in pursuit, instead of the achy, cold days of January approaching. The inspector crows had disappeared.

Ms. Pines sniffed out toward the yard. "Well," she said crisply. "I'll make it brief." (Why did I say I wanted to hear it? Had I *meant* that? Had I even said it? Something was making me suffer second thoughts—the hopeful ray of sunlight, a signal to leave well enough alone.) "My mother, you understand, was *very* unhappy," Ms. Pines said, "in this very house, where we're sitting. Our father drove out to Bell Laboratories each day. He was working on important projects and being appreciated and admired. But then he was coming home and feeling alienated. Why, we'll never know. But at some point in the fall of 1969, our mother inaugurated a relationship of a common kind with the choral music teacher at Haddam High, who'd been providing Ellis private voice instruction." Ms. Pines cleared her throat, as if something had made her shudder. "Ellis and I knew nothing about the relationship. Not a clue. But after Thanksgiving, my father and mother began to argue. And we heard things that let us know some of the coarser details. Which were very upsetting."

"Yep," I said. Still . . . nothing new under *these* stars.

"Then shortly after, my father moved down into the basement and out of their room upstairs." Ms. Pines paused and turned her gaze around toward the hallway and the basement door. "He went right down those steps—he was a large, well-built man." With her un-injured arm she gestured toward there, as if she could see her father clumping his way down. (I, of course, pictured Paul Robeson.) "He'd converted the basement into his workshop. He brought his instruments and testing gauges and computer prototypes. He'd turned it into a private laboratory. I think he hoped to invent something he could patent, and become wealthy. My brother and I were often brought down for demonstrations. He was a very clever man."

I realized for the first time this was how and when the basement came to be "finished"—a secondary value-consideration for resale; and also a bit of choice suburban archaeology, plus a good story for an as-told-to project—like the Underground Railroad stopping in your house.

"He'd put a cot down there," Ms. Pines said, "where he'd occasionally take naps. So, when he moved there, following Thanksgiving, it wasn't all that unusual. He was still in the house—though we ate with our mother and he, I think, ate his meals in town at a restaurant, and left in the mornings while my brother and I were getting up. School was out for Christmas by then. Things had become very strained."

"This feels like it's heading for a climax," I said, almost, but not quite, eagerly. It wasn't going to be a barrel o' laughs climax, I guessed. Ms. Pines had said so already.

"Yes," Ms. Pines said. "There *is* a climax." She raised the orangish fingertips of her un-injured hand up to her shining, rounded cheeks and touched the skin there, as if her presence needed certifying. A gesture of dismay. I could smell the skin softener she used. "What do you hope for, Mr. Bascombe?" Ms. Pines looked directly at me, blinking her dark eyes to invoke seriousness. Things had worked their way around to me. Possibly I was about to be assigned accountability for something.

"Well, I try not to hope for too much," I said. "It puts pressure on the future at my age. If you know what I mean. Sometimes a hope'll slip in when I'm not paying attention." I tried a conspiratorial smile. My best. " . . . That I'll die before my wife does, for instance. Or something about my kids. It's pretty indistinct."

"I hoped that about my husband," Ms. Pines said. "But then we divorced, and I wasn't always sure. And then he died."

"I'm divorced," I agreed. "I know about that."

"It's not always clear when your heart's broken, is it?"

"It's a lot clearer when it's not."

Ms. Pines turned and unexpectedly looked both ways around her, as if she'd heard something—her name spoken, someone entering the room behind us. "I've over-worked your hospitality, Mr. Bascombe." She looked at me fleetingly, then past, out the sliding-door windows at the misty snow. She frowned at nothing I could see. Her body seemed to be about to rise.

"You haven't," I said. "It's only eleven thirty." I consulted my watch, though I eerily always know what time it is—as if a clock was ticking inside me, which it may be. "You haven't told me the climax. Unless you don't want me to know."

"I'm not sure you *should*," Ms. Pines said, returning her gaze solemnly to rest on me. "It could alienate you from your house."

"I sold real estate for twenty years," I said. "Houses aren't that sacred to me. I sold *this* one twice before I bought it myself." (In arrears from the bank.) "Somebody else'll own it someday and tear it down." (And build a shitty condo.)

"We seem to need to know everything, don't we?"

"You're the history teacher," I said. Though *of course* I was violating the belief-tenet on which I've staked much of my life: better *not* to know many things. Full disclosure is the myth of the fretting classes. Those who ignore history are no more likely to repeat it than anyone else but *are* more likely to feel better about many things. Though, so determined was I to engage in an inter-racial substance-exchange, I clean forgot. It wouldn't have been racist, would it, to let Ms. Pines leave? President Obama would've understood.

"Well. Yes, I certainly am," Ms. Pines said, composing herself again. "So. Sometime between Thanksgiving and Christmas of 1969 . . ." (neuropsychically, a spiritual dead zone, when suicides abound like meteor showers) " . . . something disrupting apparently took place between our parents. I possibly could have found out what. But I was young and simply didn't. My brother and I didn't talk about it. It could have been that our mother told our father she was leaving him and going away with the music teacher. Mr. Senlak. I don't know. It could have been something else. My mother could be very dramatic. She could have said some wounding and irretrievable thing. Matters had gotten bad."

For the first time since Ms. Pines had been in my house, I could feature the lot of them—all four Pines—breathing in these rooms, climbing the stairs, trading in and out the single humid bathroom, congregating in what was then the "dining room," talking over school matters, eating PB&J's, all of them satellites of one another in empty space, trying, trying, trying to portray a cohesive, prototype, mixed-race family unit, and not succeeding. It would do any of us good to contemplate the house we live in being peopled by imperfect predecessors. It would encourage empathy and offer—when there's nothing left to want in life—perspective.

Somehow I knew, though, by the orderly, semireluctant way Ms. Pines was advancing to what she meant to tell, that I wasn't going to like what I was about to hear, but would then have to know forever. My brain right away began sprinting ahead, rehearsing it all to Sally, an agog-shocked look on her face—all before I even knew what it was! I wanted to wind it back to the point, only moments before, at which Ms. Pines looked all around her, as if she'd heard ghostly old Hartwick pounding up the stairs from the basement with bad intentions filling his capacious brain. I could lead her to the front door and down to the snowy street, busted wrist and all; let her go back to where she'd come from—Gulick Road. Lavallette. If in fact she wasn't a *figment*—my personal-private phantasm for wrongs I'd committed, never atoned for, and now had to pay off. Am I the only human who occasionally thinks that he's dreaming? I think it more and more.

I badly wanted to say something; slow the onward march of words; win some time to think. Though all I said was, "I hope he didn't do something terrible." Hope. *There,* I'd hoped something.

"He wasn't a terrible man, Mr. Bascombe," Ms. Pines said meditatively. "He was exceptional. I have his coloring. And she was a perfectly good person in her own way, as well.

Not as good or exceptional as he was. As I said, he was like a wonderful idea, but labored under that delusion. So. When life turned un-wonderful, he didn't know what to do. That's my view, anyway."

"Maybe he didn't tolerate ambiguity well."

"His life was a losing war against ambiguity. He knew that about himself and hated it. The essence of all history is contingency, isn't it? But it's true of science, too."

"So did they have a terrible fight and everything got ruined? And it all happened in these rooms?" (In other words the way white suburbanites work things out?)

"No," Ms. Pines said calmly. "My father killed my mother. And he killed my brother, Ellis. Then he sat down in the living room and waited for me to come home from debate club practice—which we were having through the Christmas holidays. Debating the viability of the UN. He was waiting to kill me, too. But I was late getting home. He must've had time to think about what he'd done and how ghastly it all was. Being in this house with two dead loved ones. He took them down to the basement after they were dead. And either he became impatient or extremely despondent. I'll never know. But at around six he went back down there and shot him*self*."

"Did you come home and find them?" Hoping not, not, not. I was full of hope now.

"No," Ms. Pines said. "I would never have survived that.

I would've had to be committed. The neighbor next door heard the two earlier gun reports and almost called the police. But when he heard another report an hour on, he did call them. Someone came to the school for me. I never actually saw any of them. I wasn't permitted to."

"Who took care of you? How old were you?"

"About to turn seventeen," Ms. Pines said. "I went to stay with the debate-club sponsor that night. And after that my father's relatives came into the picture—though not for very long. They didn't know me or what to do with me. The school, Haddam High School—the guidance counselors and the principal and two of my teachers—made a special plea on my behalf to be admitted midyear to the Cromwell-Aimes Academy in Maynooth, New Hampshire. A local donor was found. I was made a ward of our debate-club sponsor and lived with her family until I started Barnard. Which saved my life. These are the people I'm staying with. Their children."

Ms. Pines lowered her soft chin and stared at her lap, where her un-injured hand held her injured one in its grasp. Her green tam held its perch. A thin aroma of Old Rose escaped from somewhere. I heard her breathe, then emit a sorrowing sigh. Her posture was of someone expecting a blow. (Where was I when all this mayhem transpired? Happy on Perry Street in Greenwich Village, as worry-free as a guppy, high on the town every night, in love-and-lust with a canny, big-boned, skeptical Michigan girl, and trying my hand at the "longer form" for which I had no talent. Living the life of the not-yet-wounded. Though why didn't I finally hear about all this? I was a realtor. Towns keep secrets.)

"Does it seem beneficial to come back now?" I am muted, grief counselor-ish, skipping over twelve consolatory, contradictorily inadequate expressions of what? Empathy more complex than words can muster? Grief more dense than hearts can bear? I've never sought the services of a grief counselor. A dwindling group of us still holds out. Though from Sally I know what the basic mission entails: first—avoidance of the plumb-dumb obvious; second—the utterance of one intelligent statement per five-minute interval; third—simple patience. It's not that difficult to counsel the grieving. I could've said, "Roosevelt was a far better choice than Willkie back in '40." Which would be as grief neutralizing as "What a friend we have in Jesus," or "Mercy, I can't tell you how bad I feel about your loss."

But *was* it actual grief? The spectacle-grim-oddness of the whole bewilderment might require an entirely new emotion—a fresh phylum of feeling, matched by a new species of lingo.

"Yes, I think it is," Ms. Pines said softly, relative to my

house and being in it and its helping. "I was never allowed back as a girl. I left for debate club that day, then nothing was ever again as it had been. You don't think things like that can happen. Then you find out they both can and will. So, yes. It's revealing to come here. Thank you." Ms. Pines smiled at me almost grudgingly. This was the grainy, human, non-race-based contact our President has in mind for us. Too bad the collateral damage has to be so high.

I knew Ms. Pines was now searching for departing words. She was too savvy to deal off the "c" card—abominable *closure*. She was seeking she knew not what, and would know she'd found it, only afterward. If she could've framed a question for me, it would've been the age-old one: What should I now do? How should I go on with the rest of my life now that I've experienced all this? Natural disaster is adept at provoking that very question. Though why ask me? Of course she hadn't.

"Umm-hmm," Ms. Pines was heard to "say," having recovered from the brief séance she'd induced in herself, in my house, in me. She was ready to go—spryly up and out of her café chair, big patent purse swagged in her un-injured hand, a flattening-neatening pat given to secure her tam. She looked down to her green suit front, as if it might've been littered with something. I wasn't at all ready for her to leave. There could be more to say, some of it never said before. How often does that happen? Still, I jumped up and grabbed her coat. She'd performed and received what she came for, relegated as much of her burden as possible to the house. And to me. Su casa *es* mi casa.

"Many times I thought of killing myself, Mr. Bascombe. Very many. I wasn't brave enough. That's how it felt." She turned and let me help her coat on, careful with her hurricane-damaged wrist. I handed over her gloves. "Maybe I had something else yet to do."

"You did," I said. "You do."

"Umm-hmm," Ms. Pines said.

Another zephyr of Old Rose passed my nostrils. I patted her cashmere shoulder the way you'd pat a pony. She acknowledged me with a confident look—the way a pony might. It's a solid gain to experience significant life events for which no words or obvious gestures apply. Awkward silence can be perfect. The whisper of the gods, Emerson says.

"I read, Mr. Bascombe—I think it was in *Time* . . ." Ms. Pines was leading me toward my front door, past the murderous basement, as if she'd neutralized it. "It said there's a rise in world corruption now. Everyone's taking bribes. Narcissism's on the increase. We're twenty-third in happiness in America. Bhutan is first, apparently. Somebody said there's been a systematic extermination of joy in the United States." Her green-topped head was bobbing in front of me. I couldn't see her pretty face. "Isn't that something?"

"I read that." I had. "It was some gloomy Eastern European in a smelly suit. Those guys don't like anything."

"Exactly." Ms. Pines turned to me, restored to who she'd been, possibly better. She smiled—confident, self-aware—and extended her small, chestnut hand for me to shake. I gently did.

Out through my front door's sidelights, where there was no longer snow falling, I glimpsed across Wilson Lane the Bitticks' frosted front lawn. A short, round white woman in a quilted coat and quilted boots was hammering a GOOD BUY REALTY "FOR SALE—NEW PRICE" sign into the stiff grass— the equivalent of a buzzard landing in your yard. Fresh realities had dawned there, a grainier view of the situation (bank push-back, almost certainly). Mack had taken down his Romney-Ryan poster, just today, and struck his flag. New neighbors would be arriving (a Democrat, if I had a choice; married, no kids, earnest souls I'd be happy to wave to on my morning trip out for the paper, but not much more. I ask less of where I live than I used to).

"Do *you* find it hard to be here, Mr. Bascombe?" Ms. Pines said as I opened the front door for her. The air space between the storm and the coffered oak door was still and chilly. "You lived in Haddam prior to now, I know. I know some things about you. I kept up with who subsequent owners were, after we left. It's what I could do."

The round woman driving the GOOD BUY sign into the Bitticks' yard stopped and looked our way: two people, a man and a woman, talking about . . . what? A new job as a house-keeper? An FBI reference check on a neighbor in line for a government job? *Not* a family tragedy of epic proportion, requiring years to face, impossible to reconcile, with much left to accomplish and not much time to do it.

"No," I said. "It's been the easiest thing in the world. Most everyone I knew from before is gone or dead. I don't make much of an impression on things now—which is satis-fying. We just have so much chance to make an impression. It seems fair. It's the new normal." I smiled a smile I hoped would be one of mutual understanding—what I hadn't had words for before, but believed we felt together.

"All right," Ms. Pines said. "That's a good way to put it. I like the way you say things, Mr. Bascombe."

"Call me Frank," I said, again.

"All right, Frank, I will."

She smiled and let herself out the storm door, took her careful steps down the still-icy steps and was gone.

The New Normal

OUT THE HADDAM GREAT ROAD, JUST PAST five, freezing rain has turned the blacktop into after-hours, dodge-em cars. Only a few of us are braving it, our headlights glaring off the pavement like sheeny novas. A Ford Explorer (why is it always a Ford Explorer?) has already gone in the ditch, its driver waving me on with a shrug. A wrecker's on its way.

Off in the trees on both sides, immense, manorial houses twinkle through. Yuletide spruces framed in picture windows blaze outward, sharing Christmas cheer with the less mon-ied. Years ago, I drove out here on just such a gloomy-wintry night to hand-deliver a two-million-dollar, full-price offer on a slant-roof, architect-designed monstrosity that's long since been torn down, and calamitously hit a *dog,* precisely next door to the house I was hoping to sell. As with the Explorer, I went straight in the ditch, but clambered out, up, and across the black-ice road to bring whatever helpless help I could to the poor wrecked beast, who'd made a *whump* when I hit it, boding ill. (I, of course, feared it was my clients' dog.) There the poor thing lay, in the ice-crusted grass in front of number 2605, breathing deep, rasping, not-long-for-this-world breaths, its sorrowing eyes resigned and open to the snowy night—its last—not offering to move or even to notice me beside it on my knees, my cold hand on its hairy, hard ribs, feeling them rise and fall, rise and fall. It was a hound, a black and tan, some-body's old lovebug—a wiggly crotch sniffer and shoe muncher bought for the kids yet surviving on after they'd gone, and prime now to be hit. "What can I do for you, ole Towser?" I said these absurd words, knowing their answer—"Nothing, thanks. You've done enough." After minutes, I hiked up to the house I was selling, shamefaced and in shock. I informed my clients what I'd terribly done. We all three walked down to the road in the snow, but the old boy had passed beyond us and was (because it was damn cold) grown stiff and peaceful and perfect. They didn't know whose dog it was—a hunter's, strayed away in the night, they thought, though it was past the season for that. My clients—the Armentis, long since beyond life's pale themselves—felt a sorrow for me and my plight, and let me go home with the promise to "do something about the dog" in the morning. I shouldn't worry. It was a terrible night to be out—which it was. In my realtor's memory they accepted the offer following some testy back-and-forths with

the young Bengali buyers—I often recollect such matters
more positively than was true. It was a long time ago. Twenty
years, at least. The dog, of course, lives on.

I'M ON MY PILGRIM'S WAY TONIGHT—IT'S ONLY 5:10
but could easily be midnight—to visit my former wife,
Ann Dykstra, a resident now of the Beth Wessel Wing at
the Community at Carnage Hill, a state-of-the-art, staged-
care facility, out here in what was once, when we were married, forty years ago, the verdant Haddam hinterlands. The
"Community" today borders a Robert Trent Jones faux links
course, hidden from the road by a swatch of woods, the
leaves now down. A birch-bark canoe "institute" sits off to
the left in deeper timber, its lights busily yellowing the snow-
flittery night. Other grand houses are semivisible, accessible
by gates with uniformed protection. Once it was possible to
cast my eye over almost any piece of settled landscape here-
around and know how it would *look* in the future; what uses
it'd be set to by succeeding waves of human purpose—as if
a logic lay buried within, the genome of its later what's-it.
Though out here, now, all is frankly enigma. Probably it's my
age—which explains more and more about me, like a mas-
ter decryption code. In New Jersey we've now built to the
edge of the last million acres of remotely developable land.

We're on track to use it up by midcentury. Property taxes are capped, but no one wants to sell, since no one wants to buy. All of which keeps prices high but values low. (I've seen only one lonely Sotheby's sign the whole way here.) Householders of many of these expensive piles are now renting their eight-thousand-foot trophy villas to Rutgers students with rich parents—taking the long view about upkeep and wear and tear when the lease comes up.

Meanwhile Haddam itself is countenancing service cutbacks. Too much money's "lost" to wages, the Republicans on the Boro council say. The budget gap's at fifteen mil. Many old town-fixture employees have been pink-slipped in these days before Christmas. The previous manger scene, mothballed a decade ago, the wise men all portrayed as strapping Aryans instead of dusky Levantines and Negroes, has been revived—the rental company for the race-appropriate manger having upped their prices. Holly boughs now adorn only every *third* lamppost on Seminary Street. Santa's magic sleigh on the Square now has a smaller driver at the reins—the original, life-size Santa was stolen, possibly by the Rutgers students. Three prime storefronts are currently sitting empty (unthinkable in earlier days). Townhouse construction—a well-known morbid sign—goes on apace across from where my son Ralph Bascombe lies buried in the cemetery under a linden tree, lately broken off by the hurricane. Rumor has it a

Dollar Store and an Arby's are buying in where Laura Ashley and Anthropologie once thrived. "The middle isn't holding" was *The Packet*'s Yeatsian assessment.

Though every Haddam citizen I have a word with—not that many, admittedly—seems on board with the new austerity, even if it promises a dead stop to what was once our reality. "Feeling the pinch," "cinching the family belt up two notches," appear to make us feel *at one* with the rest of the world's economic downturn—which we know to be bad, but not *that* bad, not yet, not here.

Possibly I'm the only one paying close attention. I still possess a municipal memory from my years of selling and re-selling, mortgaging and re-mortgaging, eventually overseeing the razing and replacing of many a dream home. Clearly, though, *some* wound has scarred our psyche. And it's a mystery how it will sort out before the last sprawl-able acre's paved over and there's no place left to go but away and down.

My mission into the night's sinister weather, four days before Christmas, is to deliver to Ann a special, yoga-approved, form-fitted, densely foamed and molded orthopedic pillow, which she can sleep on, and that's recommended by neurologists in Switzerland to homeopathically "treat" Parkinson's—of which she's a new sufferer—by

reducing stress levels associated with poor sleep, which themselves are associated with neck pain, which is associated with
too-vivid dreams, all associated with Parkinson's. Ann has
resided in the Beth Wessel, able-bodied/independent wing
since last June. She has her own two-bedroom, Feng-Shui-
approved apartment, does her own cooking, drives her own
Focus, occasionally sees old friends from De Tocqueville
Academy, where she once coached the Lady Linksters, and
has even acquired a "boyfriend"—a former Philadelphia cop
named "Buck." (He has a last name, but I can't pronounce it,
since it's Polish.) Buck's a large, dull piece of cordwood in his
seventies, given to loose-fitting permanently-belted trousers,
matching beige sweatshirts of the kind sold at Kmart, big
galunker, imitation-suede shoes, and the thinnest of thin pale
hosiery. Somewhere, someone convinced Buck that a sculpted
"imperial" and a pair of black horn-rimmed Dave Garroway
specs would make him look less like a Polish meatball, and
make people take him more seriously, which probably never
happens—though he's officially on the record as "handsome." He could pass as the "good" cop who genially interro-
gates the poor black kid from the projects, until he suddenly
loses his temper, bulges his eyes, balls up his horseshoe fists
in the kid's face, and scares the shit out of him. Buck's carrying around a different John Grisham book every time I
see him and refers to himself only as a "first responder." (I've

seen his old Blazer in the parking lot with "Frst Rspndr" on his yellow Jersey plate.) I regularly encounter him lurking in the big public "living room"—he doesn't have enough to do, with no robberies and home invasions to get his mitts into. He likes the idea that Ann (who he infuriatingly calls "Miss Annie") . . . that Ann and I "go way back," which isn't quite the word for it; and that he and I share private, implicitly sexual understandings about her that men such as we are would never speak about, but that in the aggregate are "special," possibly symbolic, and render us both lucky-to-have-lived-this-long foot soldiers in Miss Annie's army.

Like me, Buck's a prostate "survivor," and his personal talk is the sort that would drive Ann straight to the rafters. It includes his rank disdain for Viagra (" . . . no need for that junk. I prize my stiffy, lemme tell ya . . ."); his die-hard fandom for the Flyers; the existence of a "horse pill," obtainable online that makes "us prostate guys piss like Percherons," thereby avoiding the "men's room blues." Needless to say he doesn't like Obama and blames him for shit-canning the American dream by creating a "lost decade" when it came to "little people keeping up." "He's a nice enough guy"—meaning the President—"but he wasn't ready to assume the mantle . . ." Yippity, yippity, yippity. Bush of course *was* ready. Ann, I'm convinced, spends time with him only to display for me the limitless variety of *Homo sapiens* who can easily fill my long-empty shoes. Though why should affairs of his heart (and hers) be less inscrutable than the affairs of my own?

It's not, however, the simplest of emotional transits to be driving out four days before Christmas to visit my ex-wife (we've been divorced thirty years!) in an extended-care facility, suffering an incurable and fatal disease, and with whom I've not been all that friendly, but who's now a twenty-minute drive away and somehow or other presenting *issues*. Relations end nowhere, as the poet said.

How Ann Dykstra came to reside twenty minutes from my doorstep is a bittersweet tale of our time and should serve as cautionary—if one's "long-ex-wife" constitutes a demographic possible to comprehend and thus beware of.

When Ann retired off the athletic faculty at De Tocqueville (it was not long after my Thanksgiving injury in 2000, from which I was a god's own time recovering; two to the thoracic bull's-eye leaves a mark), she'd begun keeping time but expecting nothing serious, with one of her De Tocqueville colleagues, the lumbering, swarthy-skinned, curly-haired ex–Harvard math whiz and life-long mother's boy, Teddy Fuchs. Years before, Teddy had been headed for celestial math greatness, but had suffered a "dissociative episode" on the eve of his thesis defense on rectilinear quadratic equations and been banished to prep-school teaching at De Tocqueville, a not-long drive from where his parents lived on The Shore in Belmar. At De Tocqueville, Teddy was regarded by all as profound and gentle and (what else?) super-bright, and as having "this special connection" with kids, which persuaded everybody that prep-school teaching was his true métier, rather than being a chaired professor at Cal-Tech with a clear shot at a Nobel, but possibly never being "rilly, rilly" happy like the rest of high school teachers.

Teddy, at age sixty, had never married, but had avoided the standard smirks and yorks and back-channel eye rollings about "his sexuality," by being benign. There were no rumors or Greenwich Village *à deux* sightings, or mysterious "friends" brought to faculty cookouts. Some people really are what they seem to be—though not that many. Teddy and Ann began "seeing each other," began being a couple, taking trips (Turks and Caicos, Tel Aviv, the Black Sea port of Odessa) and speaking exclusively in terms of the other ("I'll have to ask Ann about that . . ."; "You know, back when Ted was at Harvard . . ."; "Ann has a tee time . . ."; "Teddy wrote an influential paper about that his junior year, which caused a lot of stir . . ."). These are mostly things she would never have said about me, since flogging suburban houses on cul-de-sacs that once were cornfields in West Windsor rarely gets you noticed by the folks at the Stanford linear accelerator.

I know any of this only because our daughter, Clarissa Bascombe, now a veterinarian in Scottsdale, told me. Clarissa has always kept semi-taut lines with her mother—though much tauter with me and her brother. Back when it was all getting started with Teddy, Clarissa believed her mom could "tolerate" only a "platonic relationship," and that there was neither hanky nor panky afoot; that Teddy, though large, Levantine, hairy, and apparently sensual, was in fact harmless and "remote from his body" (lesbians think they know everything). And that after Ann's two marriages to two unsatisfactory men—one of them me—being with a man like Teddy (thoughtful, hopelessly reliable, obedient, occasionally mirthful but not that much, no bad history with women, a good cook, and most important—*Jewish,* guaranteeing, Clarissa believed, no unwanted sexual advances) . . . Teddy was all but perfect. Like most explanations, it's as plausible as anything else. Plus Clarissa liked Teddy (I only met him twice, by accident). They had Harvard in common and for all I know sat up late nights singing the fucking songs.

Long story short (it's never short enough), Ann retired and so did Teddy, whose mother had conveniently died at age ninety. Ann had dough from her second marriage. Teddy had his dead parents' three-thousand-square-foot condo overlooking the sea in Belmar. A charmed coming-together, it seemed, was forged for both parties: an acquaintance that hesitantly blossomed into "something *more*," instead of the usual less; a mutually acknowledged, if somewhat not-fully-*shared* sense of life's being better when not spent dismally alone; a willingness to try to take an interest in the other (learn golf, learn calculus). Plus the condo.

Ann and Teddy sent around *at home* announcements— one actually came to me—declaring "the uniting of all our assets—real, spiritual and virtual." I took note, but not serious note. As far as I was concerned, Ann had simply embarked on another new course in life, the main source of interest and primary selling point of which was that it carried her further away from being my wife and nearer to becoming just another person I might never have known, whose obituary my eye might pass over without the slightest pause or twinge. Which is the goal and most perfect paradigm of what we mean when we say *divorce*.

Though of course that's crazy. The kids see to it. As does memory—which, short of Alzheimer's, never lets you off the mat.

Following which, and after four years of landing on glaciers in minuscule airplanes, walking the Via Dolorosa barefoot, two trips to the Masters—a life-long dream of Ann's—back-country treks into the Maghreb, plus any number of books-on-tape, videos of Harvard lectures on neuro-plasticity, trips to Chautauqua to hear washed-up writers squawk about "what it's like to be them," plus four visits to Mayo to keep up with heart anomalies Teddy believed he'd inherited from his Harvard experience—following all that, Teddy simply died one morning while sitting, an oversized baby, in the Atlantic surf wearing pink bathing trunks. An aneurysm. "Dead. At sixty-four," as Paul Harvey used to say. Ann, who was on the tenth-floor balcony watching him with pleasure, saw him topple over face-into-the-sea. She thought he was playing a joke and laughed and waited for him to right himself. He *had* a comic side.

Ann lived on in the condo after Teddy's death. I had no idea what she did or how she did it. "Mom's fine," was the most Clarissa would allow, as if I was not to know. Paul Bascombe, our son—an unusual man-apart on his best day, and now happily running a garden supply in KC—maintains only a distant fondness for his mother, and so had nothing to inform me about her. Complications and unfathomables in "dealing with" one or another aging parent seem now to be the norm for modern offspring.

SALLY AND I SOLD OUR BEACH HOUSE ON POINCINET Road, Sea-Clift, in the late selling-season of '04. We'd thought about it for a while. Someone, though, just came driving past the house one day in a Mercedes 10-million SEL, saw me on

the deck glassing striper fishermen with my Nikons. The guy
came to the foot of the side stairs, shading his eyes, and asked
out of the blue what it'd take to buy the place. I told him a
lordly figure (this kind of thing's not unusual; I was always
expecting it). The guy, Arnie Urquhart from Hopatcong, said
that number sounded reasonable. I came halfway down the
steps. He came halfway up. I said my name. We shook hands.
He wrote a check for the *earnest* right on the spot. And in
three weeks Sally and I were outside supervising Mayflower
men, getting our belongings into storage or off to the auction-
eers in Metuchen.

Our move to Haddam, a return to streets, housing
stocks and turbid memories I thought I'd forever parted
with, was like many decisions people my age make: con-
servative, reflexive, unadventurous, and comfort-hungry—
all posing as their opposite: novel, spirited, enlightened, a
stride into the mystery of life, a bold move only a reckless
few would ever chance. As if I'd decided to move to Nairobi
and open a Gino's. Sadly, we only know well what we've
already done.

And yet, it's been fine—with a few surprises. The hurricane. The recession. Nothing, though, Sally or I consider
embittering or demoralizing. Ann Dykstra (Ann Dykstra-
Fuchs—she and Teddy tied the knot on one of their glaciers,
in Greenland) was not in our thinking. She was "someplace"

nearby, but out of sight. I couldn't have said precisely where. In time I knew about Teddy's departure, the renewed widowhood made somberer by the feeling (I filled this in) that Teddy was the best she'd ever have. Divorcing me decades back, leaving the children stranded, marrying a turd like Charley O'Dell—her second husband—and ending up alone . . . *all* that had been prologue to a door opening on a long beautiful corridor and to a much more cleanly lighted place where she'd ever been lucky enough to live, if only for a precious few years. I was happy not to think any of these things. Though I think them now. She was fine—just the way her daughter put it.

But then Ann began to "notice her body" in a way she hadn't. Athletes, of which Ann is a classic example, notice goings-on in their muscular-skeletal underpinning long before the rest of us, and long before they notice depression, despondency, psychic erosion or anything "soft-tissue" in nature.

"I realized I would only swing one arm when I walked down the fairway," she said when we went for Mexican lunch at Castillo's in Trenton. I now see her more, which Sally thinks is "appropriate," though I have less good feelings about it. "I thought, 'Well, what in the hell is this about? Did I wrench my arm going to the bathroom at night and forget all about it? I guess I'm losing it.'" She grinned a big, amazed, open-faced June Allyson grin across our two plates of chiles rellenos. Discovering the disease that's going to kill you can apparently be an exhilarating tale of late-in-life dis-covery—if only because genuine late-in-life discoveries are fewer and fewer.

There, however, turned out to be "just the slightest tremor," which was confined to her "*off* hand" (she's a righty), something she attributed to age and the stress of widowhood. Her penmanship (the numbers she penciled onto her score-card) had grown smaller and less clear. Plus, she wasn't sleep-ing well, and sometimes felt more tired the longer she slept. "And I was constipated." She rolled her eyes, shook her head and looked up. "You know me. I'm never constipated." When we were married we didn't talk about this little-known fact.

An entirely scheduled physical proved "concerning." Abominable "tests" (I've had 'em) were performed. "Noth-ing really conclusive," she told me. "You can't diagnose Par-kinson's. You eliminate everything it's not, and Parkinson's is what's left."

"Surveillance" drugs were administered, which, if suc-cessful in eliminating the tremor, the fatigue and the bowel issues, meant (perversely) Parkinson's was likely the ticket. And Parkinson's was indeed the ticket. Continuing the drugs, however, would keep the symptoms at bay, though there might be some nausea (she's had it) and some *bp* drops. But life as we know it—the elusive gold standard—could be anticipated, she told me, possibly for years, assuming continued exercise and patience with dosage adjustments. For all of which she's a natural.

"Who knows," she said the day she told me the whole story at lunch, "in a year they may figure the whole goddamn thing out and I'll be good as new—for sixty-nine." In later years, Ann's begun talking like her late father, Henry, a man I dearly loved long after Ann and I went in the drink. Henry was a feeder-industry magnate for the automotive monolith (he produced a thing that made a metal thing that caused a smaller third thing not to get too hot, and work better; these were days when people still made things and used machines, instead of the opposite). Henry was a tile-back, tough-talking, little banty-rooster Dutchman, not above carrying a loaded pistol onto the shop floor to face down a union steward. Coarse talk, sexual parts, bodily functions were never in his daughter's repertoire when she and I were experiencing marital bliss in the '70s. But they seem to be her choices now. I'd be lying, though, if I said I didn't miss the softer, callow girl Ann was before our son died and everything went flying apart like atoms splitting— our civilized etiquettes along with it.

The other unexpected news come to light since Ann moved to Carnage Hill is that I've learned she's lied about her age the entire time I've known her—a long time now. When I met her in New York and we were a pair around town circa 1969, I was a sophisticated (I thought) twenty-four, and Ann Dykstra of Birmingham, Michigan, a winsome, athletic, somewhat skeptical twenty-two. Except in truth, she was a winsome, athletic twenty-five, having run away to Ireland her sophomore year with a boy from Bally O'Hooley who had more distance on his fairway woods than anybody on the men's squad, and to whom she dedicated eighteen months of less than ideal life, before coming back humiliated to Ann Arbor. When I married her, at City Hall, Gotham, in February 1970, our marriage license clearly stated her age as twenty-three (I was by then twenty-five). I still have the diploma and over the years have had occasions to take it out of its green-leather envelope and to give it good, longing-filled lookings-at. I never saw her birth certificate, and she didn't show me her passport. But when she asked me to look at her Parkinson's work-up—she wanted me to know all about things for reasons of her own—there in the fine print at the top of page one was DOB. 1944! "Look," I said (a dumb-bell), "they made a mistake on your birth date." "Where?" Ann said. We were at Pete Lorenzo's. She gave the paper a quick, absent look. "No, they haven't," she said impatiently. "It says '1944,' though," I said (a dumb-bell). "You weren't born in 1944." "I certainly was. When did you think I was born?" "Nineteen forty-six," I said, somewhat meekly. "Why did you think that?" "Because that's what you said when we got married, and that's what's on our marriage license. And when I met you, you said you were twenty-two." "Oh, well." She dabbed her lips with her napkin. "What difference does it make?" "I don't know," I said. "It does." "Why, exactly," Ann said dryly. "Have you lost all respect for me now?" "No," I said. "That's a relief," she said. "I don't think I could stand that." It was then that she told me about long-driver Donnie O'Herlihy or O'Hanrahan or O'Monagle, or whatever the hell his name was, and of her flight across the sea to Ireland and the ill-starred passions on the Bay of Bally O'Whatever.

Ann was right, of course. Did I lose respect for her (if that's in fact what I had and have)? No. Does it make any difference to the global price of turnips? No. Is any part of my life different because I now know her legal age thirty years after she divorced me? I don't think so. But. *Something's* different. Possibly only a poet would know what it is and be able to set it prettily out. But I would say that when the grand inquisitor frowns at me over the top of his ledger and growls, "Bascombe, before I send you where you know you're going, tell me what it feels like to be divorced. Boil it all down to one emotion, a final assay, something that says it all. And be quick because there's a line of lost souls behind you and it's cruel to make them wait . . ." What I'd say to him (or her) is, "Let me put it this way: I loved my wife, we got divorced, then thirty years later she told me she'd always lied about her age. It's vital information, Your Honor. Though there's nothing at all I can do with it." I can hear the oven doors clanking, feel on my cheek the lick of flame. "Next!"

AS SOON AS ANN GOT THE OFFICIAL "BIG P" DIAGNOsis, which she accepted as if she'd failed her driver's test—except there was no re-test, and instead she'd soon wither and die, and there was nothing much anyone could do—she decided in brisk fashion that things had to change, and now. No putting anything off.

She put Teddy's mother's condo on the market (with my old realty nemesis, Domus Isle Homes in Ortley Beach). Like Sally and me, she auctioned all her furniture. She traded her Volvo XC-90 for a sensible Focus. She began efforts to have her old Labradoodle, Mr. Binkler, "surrendered" to a rescue family in Indiana (a sad story lies there). She began to think hard about where to "go." Scottsdale was a thought. Her daughter lived there, good facilities were on hand, Mayo had an outlet. Switzerland was possible, since there was "interesting" deep-brain-stimulation research going on, and she could get into a program. Back to Michigan came up. She hadn't lived there in forty years, though a cousin's son was a clinical MD at U of M, and knew about some experimental double-blind studies he could get her in on. She counseled with Clarissa—the way I did when I faced my prostate issues (different "P"). She made no effort to speak to me about any of it. I only got the story back through the belt-loops from my daughter.

Then one day the phone rang at my house on Wilson Lane. It was last May the fifteenth. Forsythia was past its rampant array. The playoffs were in full tilt (Pacers had beat the Heat). Obama was getting his little black booty spanked by Romney about fiscal stewardship. Iran had executed someone, and "W" was paying a sentimental visit back to DC, site of all his great triumphs.

"Mom's moving to Haddam. She wanted me to tell you," Clarissa said from Arizona. Dogs were yapping in the background. She was in her clinic.

"Why?" I said. Possibly I shouted this, as if I was in the kennels with her. Though I was stunned.

"It's convenient," she said. "Medical care's the same everywhere for what she's got." (Which isn't true.) "She says she wants to be buried close to Ralph." (Our son who died of Reye's, when people still did that.) "She said she started adult life in Haddam, so she wants to finish it there. She knows you won't like it. But she says you don't own Haddam, and she can do whatever she wants without your permission. So fuck you. She said that. Not me."

"When?"

"Next month, apparently. Teddy's condo sold for a lot."

"Where," I said, struggling with monosyllables, like a perp in a jumpsuit on a video court appearance.

"Someplace called Carnage Hill. Nice name. It's out of town in some woods. Supposedly it's the state of somebody's art. I guess the Amish run it."

"Quakers," I said. "Not Amish. They're different."

"Whatever," Clarissa said. "Don't do that . . ." She was speaking to someone where she was, no doubt about getting the Chihuahua shaved for surgery.

"It's a high-end old folks' home," I said.

"She's a high-end old folks. And she's got Parkinson's. And it's not an old folks' home. It's a staged extended-care community. She'll have her own apartment. It'll be nice. Get over it."

"For how long?"

"For how long is she staying? Or how long do you have to get over it?"

"Both."

"Forever. The answer's the same."

"Forever?"

"Whichever comes first," Clarissa hit the phone against something hard. "I said *don't* do that," she said again to somebody else. Yap, yap, yap.

"What?" I said.

"Try not to be an asshole, Frank. She's dying."

"Not any faster than I am. I have prostate cancer—or I did have."

"Maybe you two'll have something to talk about finally. Though maybe not."

"We're divorced."

"Right. I seem to remember that. I think that was called my whole fucking life. And Paul's, too. Thank you very much." She was only being hostile because she didn't like giving me unpopular news, and this was the way she could do it. As if she hated me.

I said nothing then. Nothing seemed like enough.

"Don't shoot the messenger," she said.

"Then who can I shoot?"

"I can shoot you the bird," she said to regain our moment. I love her. She apparently loves me but can be difficult. Both my children can be. "I'm giving you the thumbs-down all the way from Scottsdale. Do yourself a favor."

"What's that?"

"I already said. Get over it."

"Okay. Bye," I said.

"Okay bye, yourself."

And that was basically that.

Even before I'd turned the corner at the end of my block on Wilson, my neck had started zapping me, and I'd begun feeling the first burning-needles-prickle-stabs in the soles of my feet, sensations that now, outside the Carnage Hill gated entry—rich, golden lights shining richly through the naked hardwoods like a swanky casino—had traveled all the way up into my groinal nexus and begun shooting Apache arrows into my poor helpless rectum. It's classic pelvic pain (I've been diagnosed), which, though its true origins are as mysterious as Delphi, is almost certainly ignited by stress. (What *isn't* ignited by stress? I didn't know stress even existed in my twenties. What happened that brought it into our world? Where was it before? My guess is it was latent in what previous generations thought of as pleasure but has now transformed the whole psychic neighborhood.)

I make the turn through the gates, up winding Legacy Drive. Temperatures had risen by day's end but now are falling. Freezing rain's sticking and coating the trees my headlights sweep past. Ditto the road. When I leave I'll be able to slide down to the Great Road and sluice across into Mullica Pond. "Bascombe went to deliver an orthopedic pillow to his ex-wife and somehow drowned getting home. Details are pending police investigation." Old James thought death was a distinguished thing. I'm certain it's not.

Up close, Carnage Hill looks like an over-sized Hampton

Inn, with low-lit "grounds" and paved "contemplation paths" leading into the woods, instead of to a customers-only parking with special slots for 18-wheelers. Tonight, the inside's all lit up, meaning to convey a special "There's more here than meets the eye" abundance both to visitors and well-heeled residents alike. Nothing's bleaker than the stingy, unforgiving one-dimensionality of most of these places; their soul-less vestibules and unbreathable antiseptic fragrances, the dead-eyed attendants and willowy end-of-the-line pre-clusiveness to whatever's made life be life but that now can be forgotten. Sally's mother, Freddy, walked ten feet past the door of a suburban "Presbyterian Village" out in Elgin, then turned around and walked back out to the car and died of a (willed) infarct right in the front seat. There are statistics about such things. "I guess she was telling us something," Sally said.

Ann, though, is getting her money's worth out here and is happy as a goldfish about it. Carnage Hill advertises anything but pre-clusive. On display in the foyer is their "Platinum Certification" from the Federation of Co-axial Senior Life-Is-A-Luxury-Few-Want-To-Leave Society, based in Dallas—the national death-savvy research center. The goal at Carnage Hill is to re-brand aging as a to-be-looked-forward-to phenomenon. Thus, no one working inside wears a uniform. Smart, solid-color, soft-to-the-touch casual-wear is supplied from Land's End. No one's called "staff" or treated like it. Instead, alert, friendly, well-dressed, well-groomed "strangers" just seem to happen by, acting interested and offering to help whoever needs it. Half of the caregivers are Asian—who're better at this type of thing than Anglo-Saxons, Negroes, and regular Italian Jersey-ites. Everything inside's sustainable, solar, green, run by sensors, paperless, or hands-off and is pricey beyond imagining. Loaner Priuses are available in an underground geo-heated garage. Wireless pill boxes inform residents when to take their meds. Computer games in the TVs chart residents' cognitive baseline (if they can remember to play). There are even Internet cemeteries that invite residents to make videos of themselves, so loved ones can see Aunt Ola when she still had a brain. "Aging is a multidisciplinary *experience,*" the corporate brochure, *Muses,* wants applicants to know. Carnage Hill, following the theme, is thus a "living laboratory for Gray Americans."

I'm frankly surprised Ann's practical-minded, Michigan-Dutch, country-club upbringing and genetic blueprint would let her stand one minute for all this baloney. Her father wouldn't have and didn't give a fart for retirement. Clarissa flew in from Arizona to help her mother move in, then went immediately back, referring to the whole "community" as strange and savage. Sally went to see Ann once in October, before the hurricane. (I feared an odorless, colorless bond would form between them—against me.) But Sally came home "thoughtful," remarking it was like visiting someone in the home-decor department at Nordstrom. She couldn't imagine—she'd said this before—how I could ever have fallen for Ann, much less married her. "You're a very strange man," she said and walked away to fix dinner, while I wondered what that meant. It was enough that she never went back for another visit.

When I drive to see Ann, as I am tonight (once a month—no more—since I don't consider it good for me), I usually find her in stagily effervescent spirits, with over-sharpened wits and "good" humor that often targets me as its goat. Her tremor has "progressed" to an almost undetectable circular motion at her chin point, her glacial eyes darting, her lips movable and actress-ish, her hands busy to animate herself and make her chin more like normal and still beautiful—which it is. Visiting the sick is really a priest's line of work, not an ex-realtor's. Priests have something to bring—ceremony, forgetfulness, a few stale, vaguely off-color jokes leading to forgiveness. I only have an orthopedic pillow.

What I've attempted in my visits, and will try once again tonight, is to offer Ann what I consider my "Default Self"; this, in the effort to give her what I believe she most wants from me—bedrock truth. I do this by portraying for her the *self* I'd like others to understand me to be, and at heart believe I am: a man who doesn't lie (or rarely), who presumes nothing from the past, who takes the high, optimistic road (when available), who doesn't envision the future, who streamlines his utterances (no embellishments), and in all instances acts nice. In my view, this *self* plausibly represents one-half of the charmed-union-of-good-souls every marriage promises to convene but mostly fails to—as was true of ours long ago. I'm proceeding with this on the chance that long years of divorce, plus the onset of old age, and the value-added of fatal disease, will put at least a remnant of that charm back within our reach. We'll see. (Sally Caldwell's birthday, her sixty-fifth, is tomorrow, and later tonight, no matter what else happens, I'm spiriting her to Lambertville for a festive dinner, and later a renewal of our own charmed, second-marriage promises. I'm not long for Carnage Hill tonight.)

Ann's preoccupation with bedrock truth is, of course, what most divorced people are deviled by, especially if the left-over spouse is still around. Ann's is basically what the ethicists at the Seminary call an *essentialist* point of view. Years ago, when our young son Ralph died, and I was for a period struck wondrous by life and bad luck and near-institutional-grade distraction, so that our marriage went crashing over the cliff, it became Ann's belief that I *essentially* didn't love her enough. Or else we would've stayed married.

Imbedded in this belief is the eons-old philosopher's quest for what's real and what's not, with marriage as the

White Sands proving ground. If Ann (this is my view of her view) could just maneuver me around to conceding that yes, it's true, I didn't *really* love her—or if I did, I didn't love her enough way back when—then she'd be able once and for all, before she dies, to *know something* true; one thing she can completely rely on: my perfidy. Her *essence,* of course, being perfidy's opposite—bedrock goodness—since she believes she *certainly* loved me enough.

Only, I *don't* concede it. Which makes Ann irritable, and worry it and me like a sore that won't heal. Though it *would* heal if she'd just stop worrying it.

My view is that I loved Ann back in those long-ago vicious days all there was in me to love. If it wasn't enough, at least she mined out the seam. What really *was* essential back then (I never like the sound of *really*; I'd be happy to evict it from the language along with many other words) was her own unquenchable need to be . . . what? Assured? Affirmed? Attended to? All of which she defines as *love.*

Our poor son's woeful death and my wondrous wanderings were both sad contributors to our marriage's demise—no argument there. Guilty as charged. But it's as much what was unquenchable and absent in *her* that's left her, for all these years, with an eerie, nagging sensation of life's falseness and failure to seat properly on bedrock. Possibly at heart Ann's a Republican.

Since she was diagnosed and moved herself to Carnage Hill, Ann has become a dedicated adept of all things mystical and holistic. In particular, she's been driven to find out what "caused" her to come down with a dose of Parkinson's. Plain bad luck and her old man's busted-up genes don't provide explanation enough. Here, I fit nicely into one theoretical construct: she got Parkinson's *because* I never loved her. She hasn't said this, but I know she's thought it, and I show up expecting it each time.

She does, however, specifically incriminate the hurricane, which she considers a "super-real change agent," which it surely was. The blogs she reads (I'm not sure what a blog even is) are full of testimonials about things-events-changes-dislocations-slippages-into-mania-and-slippings-out which have all been "caused" by the storm. You wouldn't necessarily *know* it was the cause, since conveniently there was no *direct* relationship—no straw follicles piercing telephone poles; no Boston Whalers found in trees twenty miles inland with their grinning, dazed owners inside but safe; no talking animals or hearing restored when before it'd been hopeless. But to these hurricane conspirators, the storm is responsible and will go on being responsible for any damn thing they need it to be. Since who's to say they're wrong?

Agency is, of course, what Ann and all these zanies are seeking. She believes—she's told me so—that the hurricane was a hurricane long before it was a hurricane; when it only *seemed* to be a careless zephyr off the sunny coast of Senegal, which, nonetheless, heated up, brewed around and found its essential self, then headed across the Atlantic to do much mischief. Somehow along the way, due to atmospheric force fields to which Ann was peculiarly susceptible—sitting, a widow in her condo, above the beach in Belmar, looking out at what she thought was a pancake sky and blemish-less horizon—the coming storm ignited within her personal nerve connectivity a big data dump that made her chin start vibrating and her fingers tingle, so that now they won't be still. Ann believes the hurricane, which blew away the Mar-Bel condos like a paper sack, was a bedrock agent. A true thing. "We need to think about calamity in our own personal terms, don't we?" she's said to me imperiously. (I'm not sure why so many people address me with sentences that end in question marks. Am I constantly being interrogated? Does this happen to everyone? I'll tell you. The answer is no.)

"I don't know," I said. "Maybe."

Ann is not as scary as this makes her sound. Normally she's a pert, sharp-eyed, athletic, sixty-nine-year-old-with-a-fatal-disease who you'd be happy to know and talk to about most anything—golf, or what a goofball Mitt Romney is. (The Romneys and the Dykstras were social acquaintances in the old, halcyon Michigan days, before Detroit rolled over and died.) This is the Ann I mostly encounter. Though we're never all that far from bedrock matters. And she has a knack of getting me under her magnifying glass for the sun to bake me a while before I can exit back home to second-marriage deniability.

The Default Self, my answer to all her *true-thing* issues, is an expedient that comes along with nothing more than being sixty-eight—the Default Period of life.

Being an essentialist, Ann believes we all have *selves,* characters we can't do anything about (but lie). Old Emerson believed the same. " . . . A man should give us a sense of mass . . . ," etc. My mass has simply been deemed deficient. But I believe nothing of the sort. *Character,* to me, is one more lie of history and the dramatic arts. In my view, we have only what we did yesterday, what we do today, and what we might still do. Plus, whatever we think about all of that. But nothing else—nothing hard or kernel-like. I've never seen evidence of anything resembling it. In fact I've seen the opposite: life as teeming and befuddling, followed by the end.

Therefore, where Ann's concerned, to harmonize these dissonants, I mean to come before her *portraying* as close to human *mass* as I'm able—my Default Self—and hope that's acceptable.

The vision of a Default Self is one we've all wrestled with even if we've failed to find it and gone away frustrated. We've eyed it hungrily, wishing we could figure it out and install it in our lives, like a hair shirt we could get cozy in. Though bottom line, it's not *that* different from a bedrock self, except it's *our* creation, rather than us being *its*. In the first place, where Ann's concerned, I come here sporting my Default Self, wanting to put her at ease and let her feel right about things. She's never going to discover she's been wrong about me all these years. But she could be more comfortable with me and so could I. Second, the Default Self allows me to *try* not to seem the cynical Joe she believes me to be and won't quit trying to prove. *Trying* to cobble up the appearance of a basic self that makes you seem a better, solider person than someone significant suspects you are—*that can count*. It counts as goodwill, and as a draw-down on cynicism, even if you fail—and you don't always—which is the *real* charmed union marriage should offer its participants. Third, the Default Self is just plain easier. As I've said, its requirements are minimal and boiled down in a behavioristic sense. And fourth—which is why it's the tiniest bit progressive—there's always the chance I'll have an epiphany (few as these are) and discover that due to this stripping away and Ann's essentialist rigor, *she'll be proved right*; that I *do* have a mass and a character peeping reluctantly out from behind the arras like Cupid—which is not a bad outcome at all.

The risk of this, of course, is that if I'm found to have

a self and character, Ann will decide I was even more false and uncaring when we were married, and loathe me even more for concealing myself—like Claude Rains, unwinding his bandages to disclose the invisible man. Worse than a mere nothing. Though I would argue that I would be an invisible man who loved Ann Dykstra all there was in me to love, even if she never really believed I was there. In the end, it's hard to win against your ex-wife, which is not new news.

A GIGANTIC DOUGLAS FIR, A-SPARKLE AND A-SPANGLE with a gold star on top and positioned with geometric precisioning, shines out through the great beveled-glass doors of Carnage Hill. All other side windows are alight with electric candles, like an old New England church. I've steered over to the shadowy side lot to avoid the venal valet boys, who go through your glove box, steal your turnpike change, eat your mints, change the settings on your radio, and drive your car to their girlfriends'—then expect a big tip when they return your car warm and odorous.

The freezing rain, when I get out, has become hard, popping snow pellets, stinging my cheeks and denting my Sonata hood and making it easy to fall down and bust my ass. Back down the hill, through the empty trees toward Mullica Pond, late-day light is surprisingly visible in the low western sky—a streak of yellow above a stratum of baby blue. New Jersey's famous for its discordant skies. "The devil's beating his wife," my father used to say when rain fell from a sunny firmament. It reminds me, though, that it's still before six and not midnight. My happy birthday dinner with Sally still lies ahead.

Carrying Ann's cumbersome pillow under-arm in its plastic sleeve, I hurry past the smirking valet twerps, on into the big boisterous, bright-lit foyer with the dazzling humongous Christmas fir scratching the cathedral ceiling, and where all is festive and in a commotion.

The chief selling point of Carnage Hill and all such high-end entrepôts isn't that sick, old, confused, lonely and fed up *don't* exist and aren't major pains; but, given that they are, it's better here. In fact, it's not only better than anywhere you could be under those circumstances, it's better than anywhere you've *ever* been, so that circumstances quit mattering. In this way, being sick to death is like a passage on a cruise ship where you're up on the captain's deck, eating with him and possibly Engelbert Humperdinck, and no one's getting Legionnaires' or being cross about anything. And you never set sail or arrive anywhere, so there're no bad surprises or disappointments about the ports of call being shabby and alienating. There *aren't* any ports of call. This is it.

Tonight there are tons of Christmas visitors strewn

through the public rooms and toward the back out of sight—
grandkids teasing grandpaw, married duos checking on the
surviving parent, wives visiting staring husbands, a priest
sitting with parishioners, offering up Advent benedictions,
plus a pitch to leave it all to the church. There's a cheery
murmur of voices and soft laughter and dishes tinkling and
oo's and *ahh*'s, along with a big fire roaring in a giant fireplace. It could be Yellowstone. A standing sign says a "book
group" is meeting in the library, led by a Haddam High
English teacher. They're discussing Dickens—what else? I
can make out a herd of wheeled walkers and oxy-caddies
clustered close around a holly-decked lectern, the aged owners trying to hear better. A wine-and-cheese social's being
set up by the big picture window overlooking a pond and
another Christmas tree afloat on a little island. Cinnamon/
apple-cider odor thickens the atmosphere. Floors are pol-
ished. Chandeliers dusted. The Muzak's giving out Andy,
singing *hot-digitty, dog-digitty* . . . I always feel I've shrunk
two jacket sizes when I come inside—either because I feel
"at one" with the wizened residents, or because I loathe it
and aim to be as invisible as Claude Rains.

I am of course known here. I often spy old realty clients,
though I can usually swerve and not be seen and get down the
corridor of the Beth Wessel, where Ann's "flat" is, overlooking
yet another decorative pond with real ducks. Though some-

times I'm trapped by Ann's faux beau, the Philly flatfoot—
Buck—who lies in wait for a chance to yak about "Miss
Annie" and his stiffy, and what it sounds like when he takes
a drug-aided "major whiz" in the visitor's john (like "a fuckin
electric drill," he said last time). I'm hoping with stealth to
miss them all.

Though on the good side, I'm relieved finally just to be
here. My pelvic pain has all but ceased, and my neck doesn't
ache. Sally, who's performing valiant grief-counseling services
over in South Mantoloking, attending to hurricane victims
who've lost everything, told me last week she's begun feeling "grief undertow," the very woe she's working hard to rid
her clients of. We were lying in bed early one morning, listening to heat tick in the house. Expectancy, I told her, was
the hardest part of most difficult duties—from a prostate
biopsy to a day in traffic court; and since she was giving of
herself so devotedly, the least she could do was put it out of
her mind when she was home. The worst dreams I ever had
were always worse than the coming events that inspired them.
Plus, bad dreams, like most worries, never tell us anything we
didn't know and couldn't cope with fine when the lights are
on. I should heed my own advice.

"Hi," a smiling refrigerator of a woman in a large
green sports coat says (to me). She is suddenly, unexpectedly,
extremely *present* just as I'm halfway past the big tree piled

around with phony gifts, heading for the entry of the Beth Wessel. *Hot-diggity, dog-diggity, Boom!* "Do you have a friend or loved one you're here to visit?" the refrigerator says, happy, welcoming, vividly glad to see me. She's wearing beige trousers, a Santa necktie, and form-fitting, black orthopedic shoes that mean she's on her feet all day and her dogs are probably killing her. She is security—but nothing says so. Though at her size, she could drag the whole, gigantic blazing Christmas tree—assuming it was on fire—all the way to the Great Road by herself. She's not Asian that I can tell.

I am *not* known to her. Which means she's new, or else there's been a "problem" in the Community—possibly an unwanted "guest"—for which measures have had to be taken. I will not be a problem.

"I do," I say. I give her my own big smile that wants to say that a whole world of things have happened before she came to work today, and it's no fault of hers, but I'm a friendly so let me get on with my piddly-ass business—my pillow, etc.

"Who would that be?" she says, as if she can't wait to find out. Big smile back—bigger than mine. Likely she's a local phys-ed teacher picking up holiday hours before starting two-a-days with the girls' hoops squad over in Hightstown. Wide square face. Big laughing comical mouth. Though tiny, suspicious eyes and cell-block hair.

"Ann Dykstra," I say. "Down in the Wessel."

"Miss Annie," she sings, as if the two of them have been friends forever. Conceivably she's De Tocqueville faculty—Ann's replacement with the golf squad.

A large man with his back to me, inching nearer the wine and cheese layout—which is not yet all the way set up—is Buck Pusylewski. I can see the Grisham novel and the Dave Garroway horn-rims on top of his head where his greasy hair will smudge them. I'm nervous he's going to spot me and come over.

"Whatcha got in *there,*" the big security woman says. She pokes a finger right into the plastic sleeve of the ortho-pillow, making it crackle.

"Pillow," I say. "I'm bringing it."

A big I'm-with-you-on-this-one smile. "A Christmas gift," she says jovially. Everything makes her happy. People are milling nearer us. Eyes are darting my way. They know who she is. But not me, now. *What's the problem? What's going on? Who's he? What's that?* "These are awesome. I've got one." She's agreeing about the pillow. "They really ease the neck pain."

"My wife has Parkinson's." Though she's not technically my wife.

"Well, we *all* know that," the security amazon says, as if Parkinson's was a condition anybody would want. "Lemme just give you a little squeeze."

"I'm sorry?"

"Not *you,* you old charmer. The pillow. Lemme give her a little poofety-poof."

Obviously I'm getting no farther without submitting. It's not usually like this. I offer up the heavier-than-you'd-expect, plastic-encased pillow, which hasn't been opened since I bought it yesterday at the Bed Bath & Beyond at the Haddam Mall. Unwelcome Indonesian spores perhaps wait inside its factory-sealed sleeve, intent on mayhem. I wouldn't have one of these things.

The security woman hefts the pillow like a medicine ball, brings it to the side of her big face as if she was listening for something inside—an Uzi or a sarin gas micro-cylinder. She squeezes it like a dog toy. It makes no noise. Most terrorists don't have ex-wives with Parkinson's whom they visit once a month. Though who knows?

"O-*kay!*" She prinks her eyebrows as if we're both in on something. She wakes up grinning, is my guess. She has alarmingly large hands. And then of course I catch on—I'm always the last to notice such things. "She's" not a "she" but a "he." She's a Doug who's become a Doris, an Artie an Amy— now free, thanks to an enlightened electorate, to assume her rightful place in the growing health-care industry, whereas before he was dying inside selling farm machinery in Duluth. My heart goes out to her/him. My life is piffles by comparison. I wish I could make Ann's pillow a present to big Amy, and head to Sally's birthday dinner, having done the good deed the season aspires to—instead of the deed I'm destined for.

The big galoot hands me back the pillow as if she's used to strangers taking just about this long to wise up to the whole gender deal, but is happy to have it copacetic between us now. She used to be me. She knows what that's all about—not as great as it's cracked up to be. Otherwise she'd still be there.

"You must be Frank." Amy-Doris for the first time trades in the bozo grin for a mulling stare, making her look like nothing as much as a farm machinery salesman, only with breasts, lipstick and a beard shadow down her jawline.

"Right," I say, as if I'm the one in drag. *Hot-diggity, dog-diggity* . . .

"Annie talks about you sometimes," A-D says. Her mulling look means I've long ago been determined to be in the wrong about many things, and it's too late to fix any of them. It's all just sad, sad, etc. Big Doug was probably a flop selling Caterpillars.

"What does she say?" I can't keep from asking, though I don't want to know. *Boom! What you do to me!*

"She says you're okay. Sometimes you're kind of an asshole. But that's pretty rare." Doug is just Doug now. We're hombre-to-hombre. Perhaps his surgery's not quite done and he's still in the stage where you wake up not knowing who the hell's living in your skin.

"That's probably true," I say, wedging the pillow back under my elbow. Buck, I see, is treating himself to a glass of the Malbec, getting ahead of when the book-clubbers let out. Possibly he and Miss Annie have plans for later. In the distant public rooms people are applauding. The sounds of pure delight. Granny Bea's just opened her big present and been surprised as a betsy bug on a cabbage leaf.

"Hard not to be who you are," big Doug observes, nodding. He should know. She should know.

"I keep trying to do better."

"Well, you have to." Big smile again. "You have yourself a merry one, Franky. Knock yourself out."

"You have one, too." Franky.

"Oh, I'm on my way to that. Don't worry about me." Something cheerlessly sexual's crept into his/her voice. Though no more than with most things we say, do, think about and long to be true. Poor devil. But I've cleared customs now, am free to go. Free to find my way to the genuine woman who once was my wife.

BUCK, BY AN EXCELLENT STROKE, HAS NOT NOTICED me. An encounter with him would zero out my Default Self before it even had its chance. The Beth Wessel corridor, which I now enter, is like a swank hallway in the Carlyle. No hint of infirmity or decline. Nothing wheelchair width, no wall grips, no SOS phones or defibrillator paks. Illness abides elsewhere. The walls are rich, shadowed wainscot and with an aroma of saddle leather, the above-part done in hand-painted murals of the Luxembourg, the Marais, the Seine and the Place des Vosges. Ann's told me these are all re-done yearly and there's a competition. Brass sconces add tasteful low-light accents. The carpet's gray with a green undertone you don't notice and lush as a sheep meadow. Every few feet there's a framed, spot-lit photograph—a Doisneau, a Cartier-Bresson, an Atget—or at least their imitators. Sounds are as hushed as deep space. You expect the next person you see to be Meryl Streep in a Mets cap and shades, making a discreet exit out onto a side street off the Boulevard St. Germain—not the Great Road in Haddam Township.

Ann's flat is at the end. 8-B, though there's no 8-B on the door. Doris-Doug will already have announced me by wireless means—possibly a message transmitted direct into Ann's deep-cranial band width. There are, of course, cameras, though I can't see them.

I'm ready to ring the bell, but the door opens before my finger can touch the brass-and-wood buzzer button. Ann Dykstra stands suddenly before me. It's ten before six. I know where my children are. They're grown up and far away. Thank goodness.

"I've just been watching the local news about these poor hurricane people," Ann's saying, without a hello, a hug, a peck, just stepping back as if I was the grocery boy with sacks and can find my own way to the kitchen. "It just doesn't end, does it?" I take one step back, then come forward inside, and have to fight off pantomiming that it's cold as Alaska outside her door, and I'm lucky to be inside for warmth and a fire. There's no fire, and I'm not cold, or lucky. I'm simply here, with no reason to be except this ridiculous, crinkly, clear-plastic sack with its lifesaving pillow, which I've been instructed to fetch and now have done. "No, it doesn't," I say. "It's cold outside."

"I guess your Sally's over there and seeing it firsthand, isn't she?" Ann regularly refers to Sally as *my* Sally as if there were hundreds of identical Sallys, and I just happen to have one. It could seem friendly but isn't. It makes Ann seem like my grandmother. "Those poor, poor people. They have nothing left. And they're paying property taxes on homes that've washed away. I'm lucky I'm not there anymore."

"You *are* lucky." Ann's living room's like a crisp stage set, and I feel too large to be in it. (Five minutes ago I felt too small.) I also feel like I don't smell good—like sweat or onions—and that my feet have cow shit on them and my hands are grimy. Ann was always a neatnik and has become more of one since she got Parkinson's and moved to smaller quarters. Feng Shui rules all here—promoting tastefully opti-

mum healing propensities. No metal lampshades (too *yang*).
Tree energy wall colors—for calm. The bed, which I've never
seen and never will, has its headboard oriented north to con-
quer insomnia (Ann's told me). What Feng Shui has on its
mind about constipation, I don't know. The living room has
a big mullioned picture window with a single candle facing
the flood-lit woods and the duck pond (good *yin*). Tiny lights
from the birch-bark canoe institute prickle invitingly through
the tree limbs. The apartment looks like a model home in
The AARP Journal. Pale green couch. Bamboo floors. Floral-
print side chairs. Lots of clean, shining surfaces with plants,
ceramic fragrant-liquid containers, and a fishless aquarium—
small but new, and everything in its ordinal position to placate
the gods by making the whole space as uncomfortable and
un-lived-in as possible. I know there are also tiny soundless
sensors all around. These track Ann's movements, tabulate
her steps, record her heartbeats, check her blood pressure and
brain functions, possibly digitize her relative empathy levels
depending on stimuli—me in this case. Low. All are S.O.P.
for the "Living Laboratory for Gray Americans Plan" she's
opted for—and that drove down the purchase price. She can
check any of these by accessing her "life profile" on the TV—
though I can't see a TV. Ann was always a devotée of the Golf
Channel. But golf on TV may be bad *yang*.

I set the crinkly pillow sack down on one of the floral

prints and am instantly sure I shouldn't. Pillows on chairs, plastic on textiles, plastic on *anything* conceivably dilutes the *chi*.

"Did you see Buck?" Ann closes the door with a clunk. Buck the flatfoot.

"I didn't," I say, not entirely literally.

"He was wanting to brainstorm with you about buying on The Shore now that prices are whatever they are. Less, I guess now."

"Less's not really the word for it. I retired from that line of work, though." So much for those poor, poor people.

Ann presses her back to the closed door, hands behind her. She gives me a purposefully pained and thin smile. I'm irritable. I don't know why. "Do you real estate people ever really retire?"

"I'm not a 'real estate people.' And we do. A lot in the last few years."

Ann's wearing a soft, aqua-velour pants-and-top ensemble and a pair of day-glo orange Adidas that have never seen out-of-doors. Both, I assume, have the Feng Shui thumbs-up, as though she was a contemplated piece of furniture in her own living room. She's also accessorized using a gaudy gold-and-diamond teardrop necklace that husband number two picked up at Harry Winston back in the foggy past, and which she's brought out to remind me how women were once treated in a civilized world. Her hair, always athletically short, has been even more severely cropped—into a kind of pixie that no longer hides the gray, and which I find unexpectedly appealing. Her whole affect has grown smaller, trimmer, more intense, just, it seems, since I last saw her—sized down near to the dimensions of her girlhood, when I met her in '69, and we listened to jazz and took the boat to see Miss Liberty and made whirlwind drives to Montauk and didn't think about jewelry, and had the time of our lives, which just never got better after that. Her skin is shiny though mottled, her facial bones more visible, her glacial blue eyes clear and strangely bright, and her once-soft nose gone beaky and sharpened, as if in concentration. Her breasts seem smaller. She's, in fact, prettier than I remember her, as if having a progressive, fatal disease agrees with her. Though there *is* the circular tremor ghosting her chin, the source of her concentration. It may be more pronounced than in November. She is brave to have me here, since I record the progress of her ailment like one of the sensors charting her decline from the prime that seemed always to be hers. Indeed, the whole Feng Shui deal, the velour, the Adidas, the bamboo, the floral prints, the necklace—they all speak of illness, the way an old-fashioned drawing room with damask draperies, shaded lamps, full bookshelves, and a fireplace speak to me of our first precious son being dead in the funeral parlor. The world gets smaller and more focused the longer we stay on it.

I'm still gazing round the over-cogitated room, wishing something would take place: a smoke alarm going off. The phone to ring. The figure of a Yeti striding through the snowy frame of the picture window, pausing to acknowledge us bestilled within, shaking his woolly head in wonder, then continuing into the forest where he's happiest. There's not even a Christmas tree here, nor a mirror. Rules restrict such things. Vanities.

Moments of bestillment are not unusual for Ann or me. What can I get from her, after all? What can she get from me? A pillow. (She could've easily purchased it online.) All we share is the click of reflex, a hammer falling on an empty chamber, like a desperado whose luck's run out.

"Has Clarissa told you about . . ." Ann begins to say.

But I'm struck by three things at once, none of which I've noticed before. There's not one photo anywhere—not the children, not Teddy, not her garrulous dad or sorrowing mom. Not me, natch. My face is recorded only in the grainy *capture* of some camera in the ceiling. The bedroom *might* have pictures. Or the bathroom. Speaking of which I could stand a leak, but won't be asking. Old Buck's Percheron comes uncomfortably to mind.

The second *presence* (the photos' absence is a presence) is the clutter of Christmas cards on the teak coffee table— also an issue of the *Carnage Clarion,* a copy of *USA Today,* and underneath all, snugged out of disapproving Feng Shui sight, the silver shaft of a *putter!* Ann still engages in the Republican national pastime, tremor and all, with the bamboo carpet as her "green." I wonder if she has the pop-up cup that ejects her ball each time she drains one. She used to.

The *Clarion* headline reads "Life in the Post-Antibiotic Era"—something we all need to be interested in. I wish I could see who's sending Christmas cards. Undoubtedly the inmates draw lots for who to befriend. Plus Haddam merchants tapping into the money trove a place like this betokens. I see a card with our son Paul Bascombe's return address in KC. 919 Dunmore—a name he loves. He "builds" his own cards with skills honed as an apprentice joke-meister at Hallmark. Mine this year bore a plain front, inside which was printed "An invisible man marries an invisible woman. Their kids are nothing to look at. Merry Xmas. Preston D. Service." Ann's, I'm sure, is something different.

The last room-addition of note are three new oil paintings—of fruit—framed and hung on the green wall (for optimism), above the big cherrywood cabinet inside which probably lurks a big LG for when the Masters gets going in April. One by one the paintings portray: a sliced red apple, a sliced-open honeydew, a sliced green kiwi—all with backgrounds of rustic wood table tops, rough-hewn chairs, crisp white napkins, spilled wheat grains and tempting nuts of varying brown, yellow and purple hues. All could fit perfectly in a suburban ophthalmologist's office—non-confronting, non-anxiety-producing, toothsome, and straight out of the Feng Shui central office in Youngstown . . . if all three sliced fruits didn't look like glistening, delving vaginas, cracked open and ready for business. At first glance you could believe they're not what I say. But not twice. I'm unable to take my eyes off them. They're far from anybody's version of "suggestive" (I'm thinking of Buck again and his stiffy). They're, in fact, an in-your-face, front-and-center manifesto requiring those who enter here to be on speaking terms with what the pictures depict, since the person living here damn sure is, and life's too short to beat around the shrubbery.

Ann's just said something about our daughter. But I'm unable to say anything. The least wrong remark would be met with a steely gaze, as though I held certain "views" about how things should be art-wise. I don't have views how things should be art-wise. Mature women, I know, can get pretty hardware-store candid about sex. (Sally's an exception.) Years of sexual oppression at the rough hands of men, men and more men finally get brought to an end by our untimely deaths; only by then there's not much time left to do much more than talk in mixed company about gynecological issues, and hang paintings of glistening pussies on the wall in the old folks' home. Possibly that's why many become lesbians late in life. Who blames them?

Though Ann's new wall art produces an instantaneous *non-verbal* response. Faint stirrings below-decks; shiftings in the apparatus, brought on not only by the fruit painting over the TV cabinet, but by their frankness as expressions of Ann's new bedrock reality and straight-on determination to let life—hers, Buck's, everybody's, mine—be what the hell it's going to be. Put color pictures of genitalia on the wall and see what happens to your social life. It may all be a drug reaction, of course, and not destined to last.

"Did she?" Ann's looking at me displeased, her chin destabilized, her mouth drawn into a tight line of effort.

"Hm?"

I'm concentrating hard on my Default Self. Stream-line my utterances. Nothing from the past. Optimistic high road. The future's a blank. Be nice. I'm not worried about my own rudimentary stiffy. They're not as prompt as they once were—though never unwelcome. But I'm suddenly burning up in my heavy coat, as if somebody'd turned on the steam. It may be more pelvic pain beginning.

"I asked you if Clarissa'd spoken to you about Paul's 'great new idea.'" Paul—he of the mercurial Christmas cards and suburban garden-supply (*A Growing Concern* is his company's name)—has decided he needs to "grow" his business into the vacant building next door (a former Saturn dealership) and to open a rent-to-own operation, dispensing common household goods to deserving young people just starting out and who don't want to go into killer debt for a dinette set, cheap oriental carpets, a veneer bedroom suite, and fake hunting prints for the walls. Rent-to-own, Paul believes, is genius. His sister and I, however, are his silent partners and money bags. And I have done my homework on this. He has no idea of the initial outlay, about how stingy are the profit margins, and how much time he'd spend hiring and supervising repo gorillas to shadow his customers' houses and trailers to get his shit back when they stop paying—which they always do. I don't intend throwing away a penny at his nut-brain scheme, since I'm reasonably sure his "need" has only to do with the phrase "rent-to-own," which he thinks is side-splitting—like *A Growing Concern*. Paul, in my view, is best off wrestling sacks of sphagnum moss and toting flats of nasturtiums and bleeding hearts to the backs of Volvos, then standing by cracking wise with his female customers. I sometimes think of my son as being disabled, though he's not. He, in fact, pays his bills and taxes, votes Democratic, owns a car and drives it, is sadly divorced, reads books, attends Chiefs' and Royals' games, and manages to arrive to work each day in complex, rising spirits. He merely possesses what's been described (clinically) as an "unusual executive function." Thus, like most parents of adult children, I'm often wrong about him. From outer space, his life's as normal as mine, and it is enough that we love each other. Though if I don't hurry up and die, I fear he'll end up sleeping in my living room.

"It's a non-starter," I say relative to Paul's plan—my utterances kept to a minimum. My boner's stalled out already—disappointing, but a relief. My jacket had it camouflaged.

But I'm sweating inside my shirt. It's a hundred degrees in this apartment. My heart does one of those juddering things that aren't A-fib but scare the shit out of you by reminding you they could be—and will be if you live long enough. Possibly it's *not* pelvic pain.

"Are you all right?" Ann's keeping her distance at the door I've entered through. She's giving me a pseudo-concerned stare, which probably means she wants me to leave. Paul's business plans are come and gone.

"I am. Yeah."

"You look a little tissue-y. Do you want me to call someone? We have doctors here."

"It's hot as a fucking kiln in here," I say. "Why do you keep it that way?"

"No, it's not." "Tissue-y" is one of her mother's dagger words used to keep Ann's libidinous father off his game. Unsuccessfully. It's the same with me. Sometimes she says I look "fragile." Sometimes it's a crack about my "destination memory," and how retirement lowers the IQ, or how having had cancer kills synapses like a roach motel. Sometimes she tells me I look like my own mother—whom she didn't know. Sometimes it's that I "lack discipline" (about everything), and that I should take a "genetics" test to see what fatal diseases lie ahead. I have to be on my guard. And am.

"Does Fang Schway prescribe the temperature?" I massacre the pronunciation to annoy her.

"No," Ann says and smiles distastefully. "You should sit down. Take off that awful coat. Are your feet wet?"

"They're fine. I'm fine. How are *you*?" The Default Self allows questions, but only ones for which you want an answer—the opposite of lawyers.

"I'm sorry?" Ann doesn't hear as well as once she did. The Default Self also requires that I speak softly. Though sometimes I believe I'm thinking when actually I'm talking. Sally has pointed this out. I may actually have *said* that about lawyers and not just thought it. Ann, of course, knows nothing about the Default Self and would think it was stupid. Which it's not.

"How are *you!*" I say, aiming for the optimistic high road. I'm still on my feet, hot as a poker, my heart racing. I'm not taking off my coat. I'm not here for that long, even though there's no set time for me to stay. I just don't want to stand here half-eyeing ripe vaginas. Whatever their mission, it's accomplished.

"I'm just fine. Thank you." Ann's chin has become minorly stabilized. "Do you see what I bought?" She takes an appraising, curatorial step away from the door in the direction of the vaginal portraiture, regarding them as if she now saw something new she liked.

"What'd you buy those for?" I say. "They look like pussies." Lying is forbidden.

"Oh." Ann gives them a stagy moué then raises her chin in mock re-assessment. "Do you think so? I think they just look like fruit. I suppose I can see what you might mean. Do they make you uncomfortable?"

"They started to give me a boner. But it changed its mind."

"I see," Ann says and pretends to fan herself. She and I never experienced boner problems back when. "We should change the subject then."

"Fine." I glance out the picture window, thinking of the Yeti, plodding his or her slow way through the dark woods toward Skillman. Snow is sifting through the exterior light cone that brightens the duck pond. No ducks are there.

Ann sits on the front edge of one of the flower-print chairs, arranges her hands on her velour knee like a demure elderly lady—which she is. Boner and pussy talk are over. Her hands aren't trembling. I feel like a man who's just committed a violent act in his sleep and snapped awake. Though all I've done is drive out here in shit weather, deliver a pillow, and get unexpectedly hot and gamy feeling.

"I've been taking a class here called *Deaths of Others*," Ann says.

"That's interesting," I say insincerely.

"It *is*," she says. "Our topic has been whether suicide is a religious issue or a medical one. People talk about that all the time here." She smiles at me savagely.

"I think it's all a matter of space," I say, looking around to find something—not her, not the venereal art, not the picture window with the lighted pond—to fasten onto. There's really not much here, which is the Feng Shui way. "At some point you just need to leave the theater so the next crowd can see the movie."

"Elderly white men are in the suicide demographic," Ann says, "along with young American Indians, gun owners, residents of the Southwest, and people abused as children."

"I'm one for five," I say. "I'm safe."

"I'd never find the nerve."

"Most people who try to kill themselves fail, but then they're pretty happy about it later. Nobody's first choice is being dead, I guess." We both read the same magazines, though I don't see an *Economist* on the coffee table.

"Are you still donating your mortal remains to medical research?" Ann says, primly.

I know what she's doing. She's angling toward telling me she's bought a cemetery plot in Haddam cemetery—near our son Ralph's grave—in the "new part," which is no longer new. She and I used to meet there on his birthday when we first were divorced. We read poems to console each other. Long, long ago. Ralph would be forty-three. I hardly remember him. Though I can hear his voice.

What Ann *doesn't* remember, speaking of "destination memory," is that I know all about her plans and have for months. Clarissa told me when she informed me Ann was moving back to Haddam. Ann herself has told me twice. We've talked about it—though only briefly. She talked. I listened. I've also twice told her I've decided not to leave my "mortal remains" to the Mayo Clinic. As the moment when that might actually happen grew closer, it began giving me the willies. The Mayo people were completely sporting about it. "Two out of six change their minds, anyway," the woman said, clicking along merrily on her computer, erasing me off the donor list. "We manage fine, though. I don't blame you. It seems pretty icky to me."

"No," I say. "I'm not." This, pertinent to my mortal remains.

"I've decided to be buried near Ralph," Ann says in a

firm voice, hands still on knees, looking very pretty. If we knew what made women attractive all things would be very different.

I notice, though, she's biting the inside of her cheek—hard enough to tighten the skin in her soft face and possibly quiet a tremor, which doesn't quite work. The drugs she takes may make her do this. Her face looks suddenly despairing.

"That's a good idea," I say.

"Where are *your* arrangements?" She blinks. What else can I do but stand here?

"Same place," I say. "Well. Not the precise same. But near enough. You know?"

"Okay," she says. Ann Dykstra is (or was once) one of those staunch middlewestern females who, to any serious assertion, spontaneously says "okay." By which she could mean, "Really?" Or "I'm not so sure I like *that*." Or "I agree but not wholeheartedly." Though also, "Sure. Why not." Which is what she means now. Sure. Why not.

Only, when she says "okay" I catch, as if in my nostrils, the faint, rich whiff of our old life long ago. A whole world in a moment's fragrance. It is not unwelcome.

Burial plans have now possibly become the new bedrock issue—not fruit paintings, not hurricanes, not whether I loved her once or didn't. It's an improvement.

"Sally's working very hard over on The Shore, isn't

she?" Ann's thinking of the hurricane even now, perhaps of the things it caused that no one quite realizes. Sally has told her about her work, including the proper use of the "empathy suit"—useful teaching tool in the grief-assuagement business.

When Ann decided to make the move to here, she spent extravagant time and effort to "surrender" old Mr. Binkler to "a family," since he wouldn't be welcome in "the community," what with allergies and all the doggy business. The only taker was someone in Indiana. Ann insisted on driving to La Porte to interview old B's prospective new parents. But that wasn't allowed, the rescue people said. The next thing you knew, she'd want him back. It had happened before, with bad results. The plan fell quickly through, and Binkler was left without a port in his last storm. Ann then decided, after much agonizing and crying, to have poor old B "humanely put down." Our daughter, of course, went ballistic. But Ann did it, speaking of empathy. This, too, I suppose, can be attributed to the hurricane's fury.

"She is," I say, referring to Sally's efforts in South Mantoloking.

"She's a great seeker, isn't she, Frank?" Ann smiles at me warmly, no longer biting her cheek. Her chin is at it again. Though my name on her lips has made her happy. I, for this moment, cannot tolerate looking at her and have to stare around the room. It is only an instant—partly good, partly terrible—and will pass.

"She likes to help people," I say. "Always has." Don't presume the past. Be nice.

"Second marriages don't get all embroiled with the difficult first principle questions, do they?"

"I don't know."

"I've had two. Two second marriages. Both better than when I married you."

Whip-crack-*POW!* I didn't see that welling up. Though I should've. Remember Binkler.

"I see," I say. "That's good then, Ann." Her name is bitter in my mouth. For years, I couldn't speak it, avoided all opportunities when it came up—in particular when I spoke to *her.* Now, though, I can use it, as I have no reason to except as my instrument. A weapon. "You're lucky if you're happy once," I say. Not a lie. My eyes fall sadly to the pillow I've dutifully brought. I wish I could just go to sleep on it.

"Are *you* happy?" Ann says, chin mercilessly on the move. She shakes her head as if to make it stop. I wish I could help her.

"Yes," I say. I am the Yeti in the forest. A brute.

"Marriage is just one story that pretends to be the only story, isn't it, sweetheart." Her old pet name. Her pale eyes stare at me as if she's lost the thread.

"I suppose."

She stands unexpectedly, her bearing erect, hands clasped in front, eyes blinking. I think she's clenching her molars the way I sometimes do. These visits are worse for her than me. I have Sally's birthday to look forward to.

"Well. Thank you for bringing me my pillow," she says, her voice rising, affecting a smile. She turns her head to animate her face like a glamor girl. The pillow is where I left it.

"I was glad to," I say, saving a lie for the end.

"Tell Sally how proud I am of her."

"I will," I say and smile. "She'll be flattered. I'll tell her."

"It's time for you to go, I believe." Ann opens her eyes widely, but doesn't move her feet.

"I know," I say.

There is no urge to touch, to kiss, to embrace. But I do it just the same. It is our last charm. Love isn't a thing, after all, but an endless series of single acts.

Deaths of Others

Y ESTERDAY, TWO DAYS BEFORE CHRISTMAS, as I was eating breakfast on the sunporch, a strange thing happened, which was also a coincidence. I regularly tune in to WHAD-FM while I'm eating my All-Bran. The *Yeah? What's It To You?* community squawk box comes on between eight and nine, and I enjoy listening to the views and personal life evaluations of my anonymous fellow citizens—as nutty as they sometimes are. For a man in retirement, these brief immersions offer a fairly satisfying substitute to what was once plausible, fully lived life.

Since October it's been pretty much non-stop hurricane yak, in particular focusing on the less-acknowledged consequences of the killer storm—revelations that don't make it to CBS but still need airing in order that an innocent public can be fully protected and informed. Much of the content, of course, turns out to be highly speculative. President Obama comes in for a fair amount of clobber. A surprisingly large segment of our Haddam population (traditionally Republican; recently asininely Tea Party) believes the President either personally *caused* Hurricane Sandy, or at the very least piloted it from his underground "boogy bunker" on Oahu, to target the Jersey Shore, where there are a lot of right-wing Italian Americans (there actually aren't) who were all primed to vote for Romney, only their houses got blown away and they could no longer prove residency. The Boro of Haddam, it should be said, barely sustained a scratch in the storm, though that doesn't stop people from voicing strong opinions.

Other callers have pointed out a "strange ether" the storm is suspected of having unearthed from the sea's fundament, and that's now become a permanent part of our New Jersey atmosphere, causing an assortment of "effects" we'll all only know about many years from now, but that won't be good.

Many, of course, express concerns that are fairly enough related to the storm's aftermath, but that seem portentous as life signage. The sudden anxiety-producing appearance of the Speckled Siberian Warbler never before seen in these parts (what's happening?). An old girlfriend phoning, after years of estrangement in now-demolished Ortley Beach, hoping to reconnect with "Dwayne," who might be listening and harboring feelings of longing about how love broke down back in '99. One woman with a subcontinental accent calls often and simply reads a different, slightly ominous Tagore poem about the weather.

Most of these citizen concerns express nothing but the anxious williwaws that snap us all into wakefulness at 3 A.M.—a worry that *something's* happening, we don't know what, but it's bad; we could do something about it (move to the Dakotas), except we can't face further upset in our lives. Though we can sound the alarm for others.

All this diverse palaver is interesting both as a measure of our national mood and humor—neither of which is soaring—and because it makes me realize how remote I am, this far inland, from such worries myself. As I say, nothing bad befell my house when the hurricane wreaked its vengeance. Though I feel that for most people, me included, this seemingly pointless speculation allows us to share a sense of consequence with the real sufferers, feel that something can be "shaken loose" in ourselves that wouldn't get acknowledged otherwise. At the very least, it's an interesting "tool kit" in empathy and agency—two things we should all be interested in.

Yesterday morning, however, as I stood washing my bowl at the sink and hearing the first footfalls of my wife treading to the bathroom upstairs, I heard on the radio what I believed was a voice I knew, and in fact had heard as recently as just days before. This was the coincidence.

It began, " . . . Yeah. Okay. I'm just, uh, calling to say I'm a dying man here in Haddam. I mean *actually* dying. And I've been listening for weeks to you people complaining and feeling sorry for yourselves about just being *alive*. I mean I've lived with *my*self a helluva long time now—same shoe size, same ears, same eye color, same nose, same dick dimensions." (There's no "delay" on WHAD; we depend on people to self-censor.) "And I've been . . ." (a cough) " . . . satisfied with all that. But I'll tell you. I'm ready to turn the whole goddamn thing in. No rain checks. No do-overs. Since the goddamn Internet got started, nobody knows anything new to say anyway. Last year, I read—or maybe it was the year before—that two point four million people died in the U.S. That's thirty-six thousand fewer than the year before. You all know this. I understand. I don't know why I'm telling you. But it's worrisome. We have to clear our desks and get out of the way." (cough then a wheeze) "That's what this goddamn hurricane's telling us. I'm almost out of the office myself, here. And I'm not a bit sorry. But we have to pay attention! We . . ." Click.

"O-*kay!*" the show's host said, rustling papers close to the microphone. "I guess . . . there are . . . ummm . . . all kinds of ways we can celebrate . . . ummm . . . Christmas together. Let's get Dire Straits cued up here while I take a little break."

I knew the caller's voice. It was hoarser and thinner—

and fragiler—than the Eddie Medley voice I'd known back in the '70s, when my first wife, Ann, and our son Ralph moved to Haddam from New York so I could pursue a promising career as a novelist—a venture that promptly came unraveled. Eddie at that time had been about the happiest man anybody ever knew. Smart as Einstein (MIT chemical engineer), he'd laughed off an academic career in favor of being one of the Bell Labs wonder boys. His itch, though, was to get out in the world and start inventing stuff and making a shitload of dough. Which he did—a light, high-density polymer bond that kept a computer off-on switch from exploding. Eddie liked money and liked spending it. In fact, he liked to spend it more than he liked inventing things. And once he'd made his bundle, he realized what he really *didn't* like was work. He promptly married a tall, buxom Swedish girl—Jalina (a head taller than he was, which Eddie thought was spectacular), and the two of them set off barging around the globe, scattering houses—in Val d'Isère, Västervick (where Jalina came from), London, and the South Island. He bought sports cars, collected African art and diamond bracelets, had a vast bespoke Savile Row wardrobe. He kept a Tore Holm in Mystic, owned a millionaire's flat in Greenwich Village (plus his big "first house" in Haddam, on Hoving Road, where I first knew him). A scratch under five eight, jolly as a jester and handsome as

Glenn Ford, Eddie reminded me and everybody at that time of an old-fashioned movie director/playboy, in a beret and jodhpurs, talking through a megaphone.

But in six years of no work, Eddie ran right through all his insulator money, lost everything but his Haddam house, and had to sell his patent to the Japanese. Jalina stuck around to be sure the last dollar was gone, then departed back to the cold countries (she didn't ask for alimony. She'd spent it all). Eddie came back to his house, down the street from me. He had fresh offers to pitch in at Bell as a senior something-or-other, or in one of the think tanks sprouting up then in what had been farmers' fields. But he still lacked a taste for work. He'd managed to squirrel away some offshore money the IRS (and Jalina) didn't know about. He had no dependents. He concluded his acuity about women was probably suspect and that a life without that hair shirt was worth trying on. He took a job for a while as the science librarian at the Haddam Public. And when that became unbearable, he hung out an unusual shingle as the "Prince of Electronic Repair" and made house calls to fix people's hi-fis or re-boot their alarm systems or program their remotes. When even that began to seem too much like work, he decided what thousands of Americans decide—people who have halfway winning personalities, no burning need for money, no aptitude for work or boredom, yet who have a willingness to think that driving around looking at other people's houses is a reasonable way to pass a life when you can't think of anything else. In other words, he became a realtor—at Recknun and Recknun, one of my competitors at the Lauren-Schwindell firm, where I worked until I married Sally and moved to The Shore in nineteen ninety-something. It's not an unusual American story. Just as there's no right way to plan a life and no right way to live one—only plenty of wrong ways.

For a time, when Eddie was back to Haddam in the mid-'80s after Jalina had left, he became an energetic member of the Divorced Men's group, which a few of us sad sacks started out of a lack of imagination plus spiritlessness. Eddie was keen for us all to *do* things together—climb Mount Katahdin, take a cycling trip around Cape Breton, canoe the Boundary Waters, attend the French Open (Eddie was inept but fanatical). We Divorced Men, however, had zero interest in any of these activities and preferred just meeting in shadowy bars in Lambertville or at The Shore, getting quietly schnockered on vodka gimlets, nattering inconsequentially about sports, then eventually feeling shitty about life and critical of each other, and heading on home.

Eddie, though, didn't own a suffering bone. He clattered on enthusiastically about his departed wife, waxed nostalgic about his growing-up life in the Mohawk Valley, the glory days in Cambridge where he was smarter than anybody and helped the other engineers with their matrix-vector multiplications; then about the flash years when nothing was too good or too much or too expensive, and how rewarded he felt to have had the patience to discover the one and only thing that would make Jalina (briefly) happy—wondrous excess. It was Eddie who gave us all nicknames, whether we liked them or not. "Ole Knot-head" for Carter Knott; "Ole Tomato" for Jim Warburton; "Ole Basset Hound" for me. Even one for himself, "Ole Olive"—after an appetizer-menu item he thought was hilarious in a dockside eatery where we'd fetched up one night in Spring Lake, after a desultory deep-sea fishing exploit where most of us got seasick. "Olive Medley." As in, "I'll have the olive medley and a scotch." Eddie always made me like him by being the irrepressible *tryer,* something I then liked to think I'd been in my life but was almost certainly wrong about.

At a certain point, though, I just stopped seeing Eddie. He wandered away from the Divorced Men. He and I didn't sell the same caliber of homes and were never in jousting contest. He was never all that keen about real estate to begin with. He had enough money. I heard he started a divinity degree at the Seminary, then quit. I heard later he'd gone abroad with the Friends Service and contracted dengue, causing his twin sister to move down from Herkimer and nurse him back to health. Once or twice I saw him riding an old Schwinn Roadmaster down Seminary Street. Then somebody said—Carter Knott—that Eddie was writing a novel (the last outpost for a certain species of doomed optimist). Eventually I met Sally, and we moved away to Sea-Clift, after which I never thought another thought about Olive Medley—so much was I both *in* and *of* my life by then, and in no mood to keep current with a blear past of divorce, distant children, death, and my own personal fidget-'n'-drift along life's margins.

Until a phone call last week or possibly ten days ago; then a phone message that Sally heard but I didn't—although I didn't intend to do anything about either of them. Eventually she said, " . . . I think it's someone who knows you. He doesn't sound all that well . . ."

Later in the day I listened.

"Yeah. Okay. It's Olive, Frank. Are you there? Olive Medley. Eddie. Haven't seen you in some time. Years ago, I think. You live over on Wilson Lane, right. Number sixty." I recognized Eddie, but then again I didn't recognize him. He was the hoarse, rattling voice I later heard on the radio. A reedy emanation of thin-ness and debility wheezing down the fiber-optic highway. Not the *tryer* I liked once. And not sounds I wanted to hear more of. "Give me a call, Frank. I'm dying." (Cough!) "Love to have a visit before that happens. It's Olive." (Could he have still called himself Olive?) "Call me."

I had no intention of calling him. I'm of the view that calling me doesn't confer an obligation that I have to respond—the opposite model from when I was in the realty business.

Approximately five days later, however, as Sally was leaving for South Mantoloking to resume her grief-counseling duties—her "giveback" to the hurricane relief (a source of growing wonderment and low-grade anxiety for me)—she stopped and stared at me where I was standing in the bathroom, combing my hair in the mirror after a shower. "Whoever that was who called twice last week called back," she said. "It sounds important. Is his name Arthur?" Sally often starts conversations with me as if they were continuations of talks we'd been having two minutes ago, only it could be three weeks ago, or could have been only in her mind. She lives in her own head much of the time since the hurricane.

"Olive," I said, frowning at a new dark spot on my temple. "Olive Medley."

"Is that a name?" She was at the door, watching me.

"It was a nickname. Years ago."

"Women never give each other nicknames," she said, "except mean ones. I wonder why?" She turned and started down the stairs. I didn't say I had no intention of calling Eddie back. Sally and I maintain different views of life ongoing, divergences that may not precisely fortify our union as committed second-time spouses, but don't do harm—which can be the same as good. Sally views life as one thing leading naturally, intriguingly on to another; whereas I look at life in terms of failures survived, leaving the horizon gratifyingly—but briefly—clear of obstructions. To Sally, it would always be good to encounter an old friend. To me, such matters have to be dealt with case by case, with the outcome in doubt to the last.

Indeed, for months now—and this may seem strange at my late moment of life (sixty-eight)—I've been trying to jettison as many friends as I can, and am frankly surprised more people don't do it as a simple and practical means of achieving well-earned, late-in-the-game clarity. Lived life, especially once you hit adulthood, is always a matter of superfluity leading on to less-ness. Only (in my view) it's a less-ness that's as good as anything that happened before—plus it's a lot easier.

None of us, as far as I can tell, are really designed to have *that* many friends. I've done reading on this subject, and statistics from the Coolidge Institute (unfriendly to begin with) show that we each of us devote a maximum of 40 percent of our limited time to the five most important people we know. Since time invested determines the quality of a friendship, having more than five genuine friends is pretty much impossible. I've, for that reason, narrowed my important-time-with-others to time with Sally, to my two children (blessedly in faraway cities), to my former wife, Ann (now in a high-priced "care facility" uncomfortably close by). Which leaves only one important slot open. And that I've decided to fill by calling my own number—by making *me* my last, best friend. The remaining 60 percent I leave available for the unexpected—although I read for the blind on the radio once every week, and each Tuesday I drive to Newark Liberty to welcome home our returning heroes—which turns out to take up a good bit of the extra.

Like most people, of course, I was never a *very* good friend in the first place—mostly just an occasionally adequate acquaintance, which was why I liked the Divorced Men's Club. Selling real estate is also perfect for such people as me, as is sportswriting—two pursuits I proved pretty good at. I am, after all, the only child of older parents who doted on me—the ne plus ultra of American adult familial circumstances. I was, thus, never in possession of *that* many friends, being always captivated by what the adults were doing. The standard American life-mold, especially in the suburbs, is that we all have a smiling Thorny Thornberry just over our back fence, someone to go to the big game with, or to talk things over late into autumn nights at some roadside bar; a friend who helps you hand-plane the fir boards to the precise right bevel edge for that canoe you hope, next June, to slide together into Lake Naganooki and set out for some walleye fishing. Only, that hasn't been my fate. Most of my friends over time have been decidedly casual and our contacts ephemeral. And I don't feel I've lost anything because of it. In fact, like many of the things we suddenly stop to notice about ourselves, once we're fairly far down the line we are how we are because we've liked it that way. It's made us happy.

Friendship, in fact, has always seemed over-rated. Back in my military-school yearbook, if some poor cadet was ever shackled with the phrase "A stalwart friend," it always meant he was a pariah whom nothing else could be said or done for. Ditto college. Supposedly—this was also in the Coolidge Institute study—emotional closeness has declined 15 percent per year in the last decade, due to social and economic mobility eroding "genuine connectedness"—which we probably didn't need anyway. Many things, in truth, that pass through my life and mind and which I might be inclined to "share" with a friend, I have nothing to say about. All the information we're constantly collecting and storing up in our brains and that we trust we'll later have a use for . . . what am I or any of us supposed to do with all of it? Especially at age sixty-eight? What am I supposed to do, for instance, with the fact that armadillos cause leprosy? Or that dog bites are on the uptick? Or that there's a rise in the religiously unaffiliated and a trend toward less community involvement? Or that tse-tse flies nurse their young, just like Panda bears? It beats me. I could put it on Facebook or Twitter. But, as Eddie Medley says, everybody knows everything, and already doesn't know what to do with it. I'm not on Facebook, of course. Though both my wives are.

Is this "economizing on others" nothing but a blunt, shoring-up defense *against* death's processional onset (as half the jury might argue)? Or, as the other half would agree, is it a blunt, shoring-up *acceptance* of the very same thing? I'd say neither. I'd say it's a simple, goodwilled, fair-minded stream-lining of life in anticipation of the final, thrilling dips of the roller coaster. During which ride I don't want to be any more distracted than I already am.

In any case, most of my friends are already dead or, like Eddie, soon will be. Every week, my reading in *The Packet* involves—first thing—a visit to the *Corrections* box on page two, for concise, reliable attendance on setting the record straight, once and for all. It's satisfying to have *something* be correct—no matter what the subject is—even on the second try. After that, once I see if there's anyone I know who's croaked, I read at least one non-celebrity obituary—what in newpapers of yore used to be called the "Deaths of Others" page (no four-star generals or nonagenarian actresses or Negro League standouts). I do this, of course, to honor the deceased, but also quietly to take cognizance of how much any life can actually contain (a lot!), while acknowledging that for any of us a point comes when most of life's been lived and there's much less of it than there used to be, and yet what's there is not to be missed or pissed away in a blur. It's a true corrective to our woolly, reflexive shiverings about "the end." Jettisoning friends (I could provide a list, but why bother, there weren't many) . . . jettisoning friends, along with these small, private acts of corrective thinking, has altogether made death mean a great deal less to me than it used to; but better yet, has made life mean a great deal more.

So far I haven't spoken about any of this to Sally, although I mean to. She would only tell me—since she now sees the world through a prism of grief—that I started feeling this way because of the hurricane and the terrible, anonymous death it exacted; and that my actions (jettisoning friends, etc.) are a version of deep grief, which she could counsel me about if I'd let her. Since October she's been dedicating herself, over on The Shore, to elderly Jersey-ites who've lost everything, trying to give them something to look forward to at average age ninety-one. (What could that be?) Though lately I've noticed her more and more staring at me, as she did when I was combing my hair in the bathroom, and she was questioning me about Eddie. By staring, it's almost as if she wants to ask me, "Where did you come from?" Or more to the point, "Where did *I* come from? And why, by the way, am I here now?" I take this to be some unknown-by-me-yet-well-documented syndrome of grief counseling, and itself another consequence of the hurricane, like the callers on WHAD are always going on about. Sally's at present studying for her state grief-counseling "certification" and is only an "adult trainee"—though she's proved herself skillful and is much in demand at the disaster sites. But if you're a grief counselor and hard at the hard business of counseling the truly grieved—whereas I'm only here on the sidelines and not, in my opinion, suffering any evident grief—then the natural inclination would be to suspect that I'm either irrelevant, or that I'm suffering an even worse grief than anyone knows. Or third, that I'm a malcontent who has too much time on his hands and needs to find better ways to be useful. Determining which of those is true isn't so easy in any life.

On another occasion, when I noticed Sally staring at me in the undisguisedly estimating way she's lately adopted, she said—wrinkling her nose as if she smelled something bad— "Sweetheart, have you ever thought of writing a memoir? Your life's had a pretty interesting trajectory, if you ask me."

This is not true at all. My life's fine, in most ways, but doesn't have a "trajectory." It's only the budding mental-health professional in Sally to want to compliment and encourage me—a form of freelance counseling. Though less likably, saying this gives the spurious concept of a "trajectory" a pointless life of its own. In other words, it gives me something different to deal with instead of what I *am* deal-ing with—which, happily enough, is not that much.

"Not really," I said in reply to the memoir-trajectory suggestion. I was at that moment on my knees, tightening a threaded drain-collar under the kitchen sink, where the cou-pling had leaked and rotted the floorboards. I wasn't being completely truthful. Years ago, when my career as a novel-ist went south, and before I signed on to be a sportswriter in New York, I'd thought (for about twenty minutes) of writ-ing "something memoiristic" about the death of my young son Ralph Bascombe. At that time, all I could come up with was a title, "In the Hands of a Lesser Writer" (which seemed merely accurate), and a good first line, "I've always suffered fools well, which is why I sleep so soundly at night." I had no idea what that meant, but after writing it, I had nothing else to say. Most memoirists don't have much to say, though they work hard trying to turn that fact into a vocation. "Truth is," I said to Sally from up under the sink, "I've been decom-missioning polluted words out of my vocabulary lately. You may not have noticed. I'm keeping an inventory." I cocked my head around and smiled up at her from the kitchen floor like a happy plumber. I didn't want to dismiss her suggestion out of hand, though neither did I want to give it serious thought. I knew that my decommissioning words could very easily make her think I was unhinged. She already believes that because I had a happy childhood, I've probably suppressed a host of bad things (which I hope is true). Any thought of saying I was also now jettisoning friends would've made an even more airtight argument for my holding on to a "secret grief"—something I have no evidence of and don't believe.

She gave me another one of the "looks"—hip thrown, mouth mumped, brows worried, arms crossed, right foot wagging on its heel, the way you might stand in line at Rite Aid when things were taking too long.

"Will you tell me something?" Her thumbs began touching the tips of her fingers on both hands—doing it, then doing it again, like a compulsive.

"I'll try," I said, back tightening the threaded collar on the sink drain with a pipe wrench four times bigger than I needed but that once belonged to my father and thus was sacred.

"What do you think of me?"

Cooped up under the fetid sink—plastic cleanser bottles, astringents, nasty sponges, Brillo pads, colorful scrubbers, a couple of grimy mousetraps, and the sweet-smelling yellow-plastic garbage pail unhealthily near my face—I managed to say, "Why do you want to know that?"

"Things can change," she said. "I know that."

"Not *everything*," I said. "That's why most memoirs aren't any good. It takes genius to make that fact interesting."

"Oh," Sally said.

What I thought she really meant by asking such a question for no good reason was: "What do *I* think of *you?*" It's not an unusual question. Married people ask it night and day whether they know it or not, especially second-tour veterans like us. They just rarely say it—like Sally didn't. I was being routinely evaluated. It happens. But I still didn't want to write a memoir. Reading for the blind and welcoming home heroic soldiers at the airport is plenty enough for me as "my contribution"—and therapy.

"I love you," I said, as the collar snugged satisfyingly against the pipe and bit into the white silicone I'd applied.

"Do you really think you do?" Her pretty head and face and mouth and eyes were above me. Possibly she was looking out the kitchen window at our snowy back yard. Our lawyer neighbors had swagged tiny white Christmas lights all through the leafless oak boughs. Their back yard glittered and shone. They are party givers.

"I think it and live it," I said, fingering the pipe and the emulsion for a guilty hint of moisture, and finding none. I began backing out with my huge wrench.

"I love you. I . . ." Sally started to say something more, then paused and stepped aside so I could climb up, holding the lip of the sink. "I guess I'm under a strain with my clients. I feel a little incognito." She took a sip from a glass of Sancerre she'd poured without my knowing it. Tiny tree lights outside were twinkling in the afternoon gloom of mid-December. "You're not grieving at all, *are* you?" A tear in her left eye but not her right. Her wonderful asymmetry. One of her legs is also slightly shorter than its mate—and yet perfect.

"Not this pig," I said. My old Michigan joke. "I'm the happiest man in the world. Don't I oink it?"

"You do. You oink it," she said. "Just checking. Sorry." And that seemed to do the trick.

WHEN I WOKE UP THIS MORNING, CHRISTMAS EVE day, I found myself thinking of Eddie Medley. Something in his voice—the phone message and on the radio—hoarse, frail, but revealing of an inward-tending-ness that spoke of pathos and solitude, irreverence and unexpected wonder. More the *tryer* than I'd first thought, but caked over by illness and time. Even in a depleted state, he seemed to radiate what most modern friendships never do, in spite of all the time we waste on them: the chance that something interesting *could* be imparted, before-the-curtain-sways-shut-and-all-becomes-darkness. Something about living with just your same ole self all these years, and how enough was really enough. I didn't know anyone else who thought that. Only me. And what's more interesting in the world than being agreed with?

But still. Nobody *wants* to see a dying man—not even his mother. Had I thought one thought about Eddie prior to now, he'd have been on the list for jettisoning. But since I no longer *have* to do anything I don't want to do, feeling an active, persistent sensation of reluctance can become a powerful source of interest all its own, after which doing the supposedly unwanted thing can become irresistible. As old Trollope said, "Nothing surely is as potent as a law that may not be disobeyed." I could at least call Eddie on the telephone.

I therefore hunted up the Haddam "purple pages." An Edward Medley still resided at #28 Hoving Road, four down and across from my old Tudor family home—long since bulldozed for a rich man's showplace—then rife on the Haddam townscape, but less so now with realty cratered and Bush's recession that Obama took the heat for.

Standing in the kitchen, I called Eddie's number—because I could. A watery-warm, half-sunny springlike morning had turned the tree trunks damp and black and punky. The ground was sogged, almost snowless, and puddled—the grass showing-through still green, the rhododendrons unfurled as if it was March. Three nights before, when I drove to visit my former wife, Ann, in her fancy facility where she has Parkinson's, winter's icy curtain had already descended—rain, sleet, snow, and cold fused together. Today, all was forgiven.

"Mr. Medley's house," a softly resonant, funereal voice said. A man's. Not Eddie's.

"Hi," I said. "It's Frank Bascombe calling. I'm trying to reach Eddie. He left me a couple of messages. I'm just calling back." My heart started whomping—boompety, boomp, boomp, boompety. I knew already. A miscalculation. Potentially a bad one—the sweetening weather possibly was the resolve weakener, along with having too much time on my hands. As I've been told. I began handing the receiver to its wall cradle, as if I'd just seen a burglar's head pass my window and needed to find a place to hide, my heart boompeting . . .

"Is it ole Basset?" A drastic voice buzzed through the extended earpiece, trapping me with my name. Basset Hound. Why are we such fuck-ups? Why couldn't the wrong thing just declare itself without my having to dip a fucking toe in? Errors are errors long before we commit them. "Frank?" Eddie—hoarse, failing, spectral voice and all—had me pinioned via his speaker phone, through which he sounded even more back-from-the-dead than before. And nobody I wanted to talk to. A big, eruptive tussis boiled up through the line. I should've clicked off, "lost" the connection and beat it out the front door. Most people are happy with someone having *tried*. "Are you there, Basset?" Eddie was shouting. The dense webbing in his lungs made a worrisome, organic groaning noise. "Oh, shit," he said. "I lost the fucker."

"I'm here," I said tentatively.

"He's on! I got him. Okay!" Whoever owned the funereal voice—a male nurse, a hospice worker, a "companion"—also said "Okay," from the background.

"When're you coming over here?" Eddie shouted. "You better hurry up. I'm hearing bells."

Not that far away on Hoving Road, Eddie was hearing the same bells I was hearing in my kitchen—the carillon at St. Leo the Great RC, gonging out *Angels we have heard on-high, sweetly singing o'er the plain . . .*

"Well . . . Look. Eddie . . ." I tried to say.

"Why didn't you call me back, you jackass?" Cough. Groan. Organ deep "Uuuhooo wow. Jesus."

"I *am* calling back," I said, irritably. "This *is* calling back. I'm doing it. I was busy." Boomp-boomp-boomp.

"I'm busy, too," Eddie said. "Busy getting dead. If you want to catch me live, you better get over here. Maybe you don't want to. Maybe you're that kind of chickenshit. Pancreatic cancer's gone to my lungs and belly. I'm not catching, though . . ."

"I'll . . ."

"It *is* goddamn efficient. I'll say that. They knew how to make cancer when they made this shit. Two months ago I was fine. I haven't seen you in a long time, Frank. Where the hell have you been?" Cough, wheeze. "Uuuhooo," again.

The mellow male voice said, "Just ease back, Eddie."

"Okay. Owwww! That goddamn hurts. Owww. OWWW!" Something was crunching against the speaker like Christmas foil. "What're you trying to do to me . . . Frank? Are you coming?"

"I'm . . ." Eddie was way too *much* of a *tryer,* I saw—the way he always was. I never really liked him, agreement or no agreement.

"I'm what? I'm an asshole? Grant a dying man his wish, Frank. Is that too much for you? I guess it is. Jesus."

"Okay. I'll come," I said quickly—trapped, miserable. "Sit tight, Eddie."

"Sit tight?" Cough. "Okay. I'll sit tight. I can do that."

The soft voice again, "That's good, Eddie. Just . . ." Then the line was empty between us. I was alone and breathless—in my kitchen. A pronged filament of golden sunlight passed through the chilled window from the back yard, brightened the dark countertop in front of me. My heart was still rocketing, my hand clutching the receiver out of which someone had just been speaking to me and now was gone. Too fast. Reluctance to acquiescence. I hadn't meant it to come out this way. Possibly I *didn't* have enough to do. I needed to find strategies to avoid such moments as this.

A WITTERING URGENCY HAS COMMANDEERED MY DAY and self. Plans I might've had have gone a-flutter. Packing for my Christmas Day trip to KC is postponed. Practice, which I do for reading-to-the-blind, is now put off 'til later (I'm reading Naipaul—always tricky). I know I've claimed to leave 60 percent of available hours for the unexpected—a galvanizing call to beneficent action, in this case. But what I mostly want to do is nothing I don't want to do.

Still, in thirty minutes, I'm out the door, to my car and the moist, milky winter-warm morning. A big L-10 is just whistling over—so low I can almost see tiny faces peering down, quizzical, as New Jersey's middle plain rises to greet them. On our rare ocean-wind days, the Newark approaches shift westward, and the in-bounds from Paris and Djibouti lumber in at tree tops, so that we might as well live in Elizabeth. The current warm snap also denotes new weather moving across from Ohio, readying a jolly white Christmas for wise stay-at-homes, though a nightmare for the imprudent— me—flying on Christmas Day, using miles.

My Christmas-trip idea, in its first positive iteration, was for a festive family fly-in to ole San Antone (my life-long dream is to visit the Alamo—proud monument to epic defeat and epic resilience), all bankrolled by me, including a stay at the Omni, an early-season Spurs' game, capped off by a big Christmas *almuerzo* at the best "real Mexican" joint money could buy—La Fogata, on Vance (I did my research). Others could then wander the River Walk and do as others wanted, while Sally and I took a driving trip up to the Pedernales and the LBJ shrines—locales of dense generational interest and meaning; then backtrack through Austin so I could see the Charles Whitman Tower from sixty-six, then be climbing onto Southwest by the twenty-eighth, headed home to the Garden State.

None of which worked out. Sally decided the grievers of South Mantoloking needed her "at this critical holiday season" more than I did. Clarissa, in Scottsdale, is currently having "issues" with her brother, who means to expand his garden-supply business to include a rent-to-own outlet in the building next door—which she and I oppose. They're not talking. In the face of our opposition, Paul has declared the Alamo (the "à la mode" in his parlance) to be an historical bad joke and waste of time and blood, and that no one should ever enter Texas in the first place. Instead, he's insisted I come to KC, where he can grill me about his rent-to-own theories. Not very appealing, to be honest. Though it's what I've decided, since there are days (which must be true for all fathers) when I badly miss my surviving son—as strange a man as he is and will be. Plus, I don't want to be home alone on Christmas.

I am, though, questioning my wisdom this morning—

with the possibility of a weather lockdown at Newark and snow up to my butt. In the world today, no one should experience a wittering urgency without knowing there's a cause somewhere close by, even if you can't see it.

My Wilson Lane neighborhood, as I drive down to the Choir College and turn toward Haddam's west end, is a far cry from the days when I flogged houses here and my kids were young. Although the casual observer might not notice much has been altered.

Most of the small, frame, President-streets houses, on their manageable fifty-foot lots, look as they have since the boomer '90s. Though residential stock has slowly begun passing into less confident hands—the banks, absentee owners, weekenders from Gotham, and property managements. They mostly keep things ship-shape, but not as if every owner lived in every abode the way they used to.

And more change is already in evidence. A code variance for a chiropractor. A single-hand lawyer's-office conversion where a widow recently lived and died. A holistic wellness center with Pilates and Reiki gurus inside. An online travel agent and copy shop. Following which, it's a quick descent to a head shop, a T-shirt emporium, a RadioShack, and a tattoo/nail salon. Mixed use—the end of life as we know it. Though my bet is I'll be in my resting place before that bad day dawns. If there's a spirit of one-ness in my b. '45 generation, it's that we all plan to be dead before the big shit train finds the station.

In the eight years since Sally and I arrived back from Sea-Clift, we haven't much become acquainted with our neighbors. Very little gabbing over the fence to share a humorous "W" story. Few if any spontaneous invitations in for a Heineken. No Super Bowl parties, potlucks, or house-warmings. Next door might be a Manhattan Project pioneer, Tolstoy's grand-daughter, or John Wayne Gacy. But you'd hardly know it, and no one seems interested. Neighbors are another vestige of a bygone time. All of which I'm fine with.

However, just after Thanksgiving, a month ago, I found a letter in my mailbox, hand-addressed in pencil to RESI-DENT. On a sheet of coarse, lined, drugstore bond, in block letters was a message that said, "Sir or Madame. My name is Reginald P. Oakes. I was convicted of carnal knowledge of a juvenile in 2010. I now reside at 28 Cleveland Street, Haddam, New Jersey. 085__."

"They *have* to do that," Sally said, finishing a client report at the dining room table. Being a grief counselor-in-training, she's now versed in all things publicly protective and child sensitive. "It's part of their release deal. If you petition the court, he'll have to move. It's pretty unfair, if you ask me."

I took little note, but not *no* note.

Not long before that, in August, another letter turned

up, this one addressed to me on official blue-and-white American Express letterhead. It contained a brand-new AMEX card in the name of a Muhammad Ali Akbar, who as far as I could find out, no one here-around knew. This letter I hand-delivered to the Haddam PD, but have since heard nothing back. Twice then in the fall, the Garden State Bank, which has foreclosed on two houses on our block, authorized the same police to stage mock hostage extractions in one of the now-empty homes, just a few doors down. We all stood in our yards and watched as SWAT units broke in the front door of what had been a former Democratic mayor's daughter's townhouse, until she got divorced and booted out. There was a lot of wild shouting and bullhorns blaring and lights flashing and sirens whooping, plus the appearance of some kind of robot. After which a tiny African American woman (Officer Sanger, whom we all know) was led out in handcuffs and driven away to "safety."

How these occurrences foretell changes that'll eventuate in a Vietnamese massage becoming my new neighbor is far from clear. But it happens—like tectonic plates, whose movement you don't feel 'til it's the big one and your QOL goes away in an afternoon.

All signs bear watching: how many visits Animal Control makes to your block in a month; whether the lady across the street marries her Jamaican gardener to secure him a green card; how often a barking dog appears on the roof next door—like in Bangalore or Karachi; how many Koreans of the same family grouping buy in, in a two-year period. Last week I walked out to sprinkle sno-melt on the walk so the postman, who happens to be named Scott Fitzgerald, wouldn't slip and end up suing me. And right in the crusty grass I found someone's upper plate—as intimate and shocking as a human body part. Who knows who'd left it there—as a joke, out of frustration, as an act of vengeance, or just as a sign of things to come that can't at this late stage in civilization be interpreted. My old, departed friend Carter Knott (an Alzheimer's casualty who one winter night went kayaking off Barnegat Lighthouse and never found the shore again) used to say to me: "The geniuses are the people who spot the trends, Frank, the ones who see Orion where the rest of us assholes just see a bunch of pretty stars." What's trending around me now and here—my own neighborhood—I'm sure I'll never have the time or genius to figure out.

I DO NOTICE, AS I CROSS HODGE ROAD TO THE WELL-heeled west side—my window down to take in the unseasonable springtime breezes—that a briny-sulfur tang now floats about, as if the hurricane's insult has vaporized and come inland, two months on, leaving a new stinging *atmosphere* everyone senses but would just as soon not. Possibly the radio callers *aren't* so crazy after all.

Eddie Medley's big, in-town mansion at #28 is, to my eye, little changed from his glory days of invention, mammon, the Swedish wife, boats, cars, voyages—the grinning, well-heeled devil-may-care-when-everybody-was-your-pal. Eddie's is one of the old, lauded west-side ramblers, far back from the street and visible only in peeks through the privet and yews and rhododendrons the driveway winds through. Ann used to covet Eddie's house as her "perfect house," disparaging our old Tudor half-timber as kitsch—which it was, and which was the idea. (I loved it and mourned when it got hauled down by a family of right-wing, proto-Tea-Party Kentucky brown-shirts, who backed David Duke for President and kept a private army at the ready in the coal-mining hills, but who ultimately grew demoralized by how many Jews there were up the seaboard—plenty—and retreated back to Ironville where white people run everything.)

Eddie's house indeed rambles all the hell around into the trees in "wings" that extend from the pillared and pedimented Greek Revival original home place. The add-ons were built by successive generations of owners, so kids could have their own "space," so phalanxes of new wives could have a dance-and-yoga studio, a dark room, a gallery for the mezzo-American collection, a solarium, a herbarium, a print shop, a greenhouse, and a screening room. Plus, a granny apartment, and more than one neat little place just to be quiet in and think, while the men of the house were off in Hong Kong and Dubai doing mammoth deals to bring in tons of money to pay for everything. It's not an unusual house history on the west side. Though the unhappy result is that few who abide here now have much of a toehold on where they live—the way real people used to. Money sweeps in, money sweeps out. Only the houses—grand and still and equity-rich—testify to the lives that pass through.

Eddie, however, is an exception, having owned his big larruping, cobbled-up pile since the '70s, when he paid 350K and could now (Eddie's "now," of course, is about to transfer to "then") bring 4 mil and maybe more. Though as I come to a stop in the pea-gravel front turnaround that encircles a lump of female-inspired bronze sculpture that could be a Henry Moore, I see his house has suffered considerable "deferred maintenance"—realtor lingo for physical decline destined to inflict wounds to the wallet. Eddie's house could use a paint job, a new roof, new sills and soffits, and some repointing in its brick foundation and chimneys. The Greek columns could stand new pedestals. The rambling wings are also showing subsidence signs, suggesting unaddressed water issues (or worse). Four million might be optimistic. Not that Eddie gives a shit. Though if an emir or an oligarch or an

African warlord with a Wharton MBA bought the place, the first thing he'd do would be to level it, the way the rabid Kentuckians leveled my old house, flattening the past and all my old dreams in a day.

As I'm climbing out of my car, Eddie's white front door unexpectedly opens back and out toddles Fike Birdsong—a human I do *not* want to see, and giving an unhappy twist to the words *a sight for sore eyes*. Fike's dented old Cherokee, I now see at the house side of the driveway, where I hadn't noticed it but should've.

Fike is a minister-minus-portfolio; an eager-beaver balls-of-his-feet Alabama Princetonian and Theological Institute grad, who's always popping up when you don't want him to, and who nobody in his right mind would trust with a congregation of goats. Fike's lurked around Haddam for years, doing the morning devotional on WHAD, filling in at Newark airport as a "Delta chaplain" (plane-crash duties), and officiating at funerals and weddings where nobody has any beliefs but wants a church send-off anyway. He's also an egregious Romney-Ryan supporter (his car bears their sticker), and since the election behaves as if "Mitt" actually won, only the rest of us are too stupid to know it.

Fike's also a preposterous in-line skater. I often see him whizzing down Seminary Street in an electric green *zoom* helmet, dick-packer tights way too small for his bulgy dimensions, and orange-and-black Princeton knee pads. He's been married multiple times, has kids scattered all over, lives in a dismal little bachelor rental in Penns Neck, and always acts as if he and I are old friends. Which we're not. Fike never ventures near spiritual matters with me, preferring to steer as near as possible to right-wing politics, where his heart is, and which he may believe we share. You know people in a town this size, whether you know them or not. I'm certain Fike's never come closer to a "godly experience" than a duck has to driving a school bus. He is a typical southerner in this way. Seeing him here makes me want to jump in my car and speed away.

"Our old friend's not doin' *real* good in there, Frank. I'm sorry to say it." Fike begins nodding in his world-weary way before we're close enough to converse, given the hushed tones he considers appropriate. Fike knows I'm a southerner and enjoys putting it on, as if it makes me feel at ease. It doesn't. "He's sorely sufferin'. I tried to render myself available to hear his confession. But he's standing firm there." Fike, of course, is not a Catholic. He's Pleistocene C-of-C'er, but wouldn't let that get in the way. There's a creepy tone to everything he says—a flicker in the fleshy, twitchy corners of his mouth signals it: all this spirituality bidnus is really pretty goddamn funny, only I and you are the only ones who understand it: God. Death. Grief. Salvation. A hoot when you really think about it. Fike's morning devotionals all have this tickle-your-funny-bone, cloyingly Christian pseudo-irreverence calculated to paint God Almighty as just one of the boys. "It's not always gay being gay." (I listen in if I'm up at six, just to piss myself off.) "How close is square one to cloud nine?" "Don't make me come down there!" (One of his few indistinct references to the deity.) "It's a slippery slope to the moral high ground." I'm sure Fike thinks these make people like him and be more apt to let him perform non-denominational grave-side services. Ultimately, though, Fike's no more sincere about god than an All-State agent.

"How do you happen to be here, Fike," I say, disguising my distaste with the semblance of curiosity. Fike's barely medium stature, wears black horn-rims, a cheap black suit, has his hair side-parted in an ear-lowering brush cut, and carries a black ministerial briefcase containing, I'm sure, the shabby tricks of his trade—holy water vial, a few stale *hosts,* an aspergillum, an assortment of crosses, a maniple, an exorcist kit, plus a value-pak of spearmint and a copy of *Men's Health.* Just for today, he's also wearing a one-faith-fits-all purple priest's collar camouflaging whatever mischief he's up to here.

"Frank, you might know, I've been Eddie's spiritual adviser for some time. At *his* invitation." Fike elevates visibly on the balls of his feet, as if what he's said has made him taller.

"Why does Eddie *need* a spiritual adviser?"

"That's a question you have to ask *your* self, Frank." Fike's mouth-corners twitch with seamy significance. He's gotten fatter since I last saw him. His round cheeks are pink and unsatisfyingly glowing, as if he's pinched himself just before stepping outside.

"I won't be asking myself that, Fike. I watch a good bit of TV now. That's enough."

"I see your good wife over in Mantoloking, Frank. I perform some counseling over there. She's doing sovereign work, I can promise you. A lot of grief's left unexpressed after the storm. You probably know that."

"So she tells me." If Fike says my name one more time I may grab him by his idiot collar and drag him to the ground. Much more than I dislike Fike, he embarrasses me. Though I'm aware embarrassment owes to the fear that some quality in him is identical to some quality in me that I like. The appearance of tolerance. I'm sure Eddie only keeps Fike around for laughs.

A pair of big black crows up in Eddie's giant elephant-skin copper beech begins cawing noisily down at us. Out on Hoving Road I hear the grumble of the TRASH-8-8-8 truck the Boro now outsources our garbage to. Service here is better than where I live. I again hear the bells Eddie heard—gong, gonging, *Joy to the world, the Lord is come . . .*

"Tell me something, Fike." I say this because I can't *not*.

"What the hell's wrong with just grieving by yourself? When my son died, I managed my own grief." Misery, I've learned, doesn't really love company, just like nature doesn't abhor a vacuum. Nature, in fact, accommodates vacuums pretty well.

"Frank, do you know Horace Mann?" Fike's pink tongue tip makes a roguish tour of his lips. He's not going to answer me. I don't really want him to, anyway.

"Not personally. No."

"Well. Horace Mann, Frank, said—or wrote—I was just reading his biography last night, trying to write a Christmas devotional with some meat on its bones. Horace Mann said, 'Unless you've done something for humanity, you should be afraid to die.' I thought that was interesting. Doing something for humanity." Fike crosses his chubby arms over his fat brief-case and hugs it like a life preserver, then makes his mouth into a little peachy pucker as if he's waiting for what I might say next. Fike's fingers are slender and pretty like a girl's and have trimmed, pink, well-tended nails. He is a rare breed of asshole.

The big crows caw at us again where we stand on the damp pea gravel. Each of us, I'm sure, wants the other to go away.

"I'll think about that, Fike. Thanks."

"You know, Frank. When I think about Governor Romney versus this President we currently have—which I do a lot—I think I know which of them fears death the most. As

I'm sure you do." Fike nods. His moist mouth corners flicker up then down then up. He's registering, he believes, a delicious little victory. I look at the bumper of my Sonata to see if I still have my Obama sticker. I mostly do. I started scraping it off after Thanksgiving then forgot. Fike, the little pastoral weasel, has observed it—which is why he brings up "this President." It is his only religion. Politics and dough. God's just the day job.

I say nothing, just stare back at him. If "this President" fears death it's because he knows the Fike Birdsongs of the world are gunning for him. I once saw Fike stepping out of the Vietnamese massage establishment out on Route 1—a flat-roofed, windowless, cinder-block bunker—formerly a Rusty Jones—with its lighted sign-on-wheels out front. KumWow. I could make a cheap reference to it now. Fike could work it into his Yuletide message. What Horace Mann would say about KumWow? A solace for our unexpressed griefs? Only, it's Christmas Eve. And even for a non-believer, desist is easier than engage. Though I wonder what Fike's father thinks of him, down in Fairhope. Fike's about my son Ralph's age—or would be.

Above his little purple priest's collar, Fike stares at me hungrily. Silence is the best defense against non-entities—let them become insubstantial, like a retreating fog. I sniff the sharp-sulfurous sea tang blown inland from the shore. Hazards ride its whispering waves.

"Frank. Don't act too shocked when you see poor ole Eddie. Okay? He's looking rough. Underneath he's still Eddie, though. He'll really appreciate you coming." Fike's become confident again—all by himself. To prove it he sets his mouth into a downward-curving parabola, like a banker nullifying a loan extension. *Bong, bong, bong. Let e-e-e-vry hear-ar-art, pre-pa-re hi-um roo-ooo-oom, and heavin 'n nachure sing . . .*

"I'll try to steel myself, Fike."

"Maybe I'll see you on the radio, Frank?" Fike hugs his briefcase tighter, backing away from me, as if we were in a narrow alley out here. "I like that Narpool you've been read-ing on the air. Though not that much happens there, wouldn't you say?"

"That's the point, Fike. You have to be available to what's not evident."

"Look out, now! That's my line of work, Frank. Evi-dence of things unseen, etc. Hebrews Two." This pleases him. He brightens supremely, backing away still. We've found our point of assent—in the unseen—a sacred accord that will let us go our separate ways to Sunday—which we do. Blessedly.

EDDIE'S FRONT DOOR IS ONCE AGAIN PULLED OPEN, this time by a big, pillowy black woman in tight red toreadors with little green Christmas trees printed all over them. She gives me an indifferent look and stands back for me to come in. She's wearing a green scrub-in smock and cracked white nurse's shoes her big feet have badly stressed. A stethoscope hangs off her neck. A yellow sponge is in one hand, as if she's been doing dishes. She smells of peppermint.

"I'm Frank Bascombe," I say, half whispering. "I think Eddie's expecting me."

"All right," she says as I come in. "Finesse," she says, which I take to be her name. "I'm his hospice nurse. He been kickin' up dust, waitin' for you." She steps off, leading me to the right, out of the shadowy foyer and the main house's front parlor—Greek Revival, pocket doors, bookcases, a sunny breakfast nook visible through doors to the back. Everything in the original part's been *done* in ultramodern-'70s style—shiny tube-steel and leather chairs, the walls hand-painted in bold, jagged red-and-green striping and hung with large black-and-white photographs of the Serengeti, wattle huts, Mount K, an immense and motionless river with rhinos cavorting, and lots of artifacts around—a ceremonial zebra-skin drum-table, spears clustered in an elephant's-foot umbrella stand, walls of hollow-eyed masks and shields and breastplates made of leopard fur—the dark continent's designer side. Everything's silent and pristine. No life's transpired here, possibly, since the lady of the house flew back to square-head land, leaving it as her monument.

Finesse's size and swaying stride create a peppermint airstream, where I'm following behind. "I thought that funny l'il preacher—whatever *he* was—wasn't ever gonna leave," she's saying as if she and I know each other. "*Fice.* Idn't that a dog's name? I don't b'lieve I met *you.* I *did* meet some of them." She's leading me through a dark screening theater and on into a paneled man-study with *Vanity Fair* prints, crossed wooden tennis rackets, the (apparently) complete Harvard Classics and a big Cape buffalo's head staring somberly down off the wall. We pass then into a *club* room—snooker table, highboy chairs, Tiffany lamps, deep-cranberry walls, cue racks, chalks, a triangle of red balls on a perfect green nap. Again, nothing seems in use. Plans were made. Plans abandoned.

"I'm an *old* friend." I'm barely keeping up. We pass through double doors to a small, expensively lit seafaring chamber—brass-framed charts, brass fixtures, brass telescopes, windlasses, monkeys' fists, boat hooks, belaying pins, fife rails—everything but an oubliette. Plus walls of big blow-up glossies of Eddie on his beloved Tore Holm yawl, the *Jalina,* christened to honor the departed wife and long-ago lost to creditors. Eddie is distinctive (if miniaturized) as the doughty helmsman of the big seventy-footer, bowsprit (or whatever) to the bluster and spray, sails bellied, the commodore in white ducks and shades, deliriously happy, Jalina clutching his shoulders, her straight blondy tresses streaming behind (revealing a face a bit too small for *her* shoulders). I could never prize anything so much. A career selling houses lets you know you can live with a lot less than you think.

"Okay, lemme just say this," Finesse says, coming about just as we're about to pass through another double doors, possibly to Eddie's dying room, where his dying days are upon him. Finesse would be *my* choice for nurse when the time arrives—big as a tractor, strong as a bison, bristling with authority and competence, yet also with outsized no-nonsense empathies acquired in a lifetime of shepherding rich white people out of this teary vale with a minimum of bother. Possibly she has a business card.

Finesse's protruding jaundice-y eyes and expansive forehead lean forward at me now as important signifiers. "Mr. Medley is *very* ill. He's 'bout dead." She elevates her chin, her plush mouth in a tight, pious line to represent 1. Gravity; 2. Respect; 3. Solemnity; 4. Sorrow; 5. Consideration; 6. Submission; 7. Candor; 8. Lament. Plus a hundred inexpressibles that come into play (or might) when we elect to face the final hours of another.

"I know," I say, meekly. Now that I'm in death's maritime anteroom, I want to be a hundred miles away from it. "Eddie announced he was dying on the radio."

"Okay. I know 'bout all that foolishness." Finesse's maximum breasts expand almost audibly against her nurse's smock, advancing her stethoscope disk out toward me then back again. "But he's happy. He don't mind it. His brain's goin' and goin'. So you don't have to be sorrowing. Because *he's* not."

"Okay," I say. "I don't expect to be here long." I hope. Finesse, I see, wears a thin gold wedding band barely visible deep in her finger flesh. Somewhere there's a Mr. Finesse. Trenton, no doubt. A tough, wiry, agreeable man she bosses around and reminds every day how things are going to be in this world and the next. I can only imagine how much he loves her—all there is to love.

"You stay just as long in there as you want to," Finesse says. She still has the yellow sponge in hand. "It ain't like you makin' him tired. He's already tired."

"Okay."

"Then, here we all go." She reaches for the knob, pushes back the door to reveal . . . Eddie (I guess) . . . propped up in bed, looking not like Glenn Ford but like a little bespectacled monkey who's reading *The Economist*.

"Who's that?" the tiny creature who might be Eddie says, as if alarmed, his mouth making a shocked, half-open, toothy grimace, his brow furrowing above a pair of reading glasses, his little spidery fingers setting *The Economist* out of the way so he can see. He looks terrifying and terrified. Almost nothing Eddie-ish is recognizable.

"Who you *think* it is?" Finesse says archly. "Yo' ole man-friend who called you up this mornin'."

"Who?" Eddie croaks.

"It's Frank, Olive." With overpowering reluctance, I make an awkward step-in through the door, my gaze fixed on him. My mouth and cheeks are working at a smile that won't quite materialize. I stuff my hands in both pants pockets as if they're cold. I'm already doing this badly. I lack the skill set. Who'd want it?

"Now don't start actin' like you don't know who it is," Finesse says bossily, moving with casual, mountainous author-ity toward the foot of the metal bed brought in by her hospice team. Part of the death package. Brusquely, she re-situates the metal drip stand Eddie's connected to and that's delivering clear fluid out of a collapsible sachet into a port on the back of his cadaverous left hand. Eddie's covered to his chin in a hospital-blue sheet and is barely detectable beneath it.

"Okay, okay. I know." He coughs without flailing an arm over his mouth, which would be better.

"And cover up yo' mouth, Mr. Nasty!" Finesse gives the minuscule Eddie a frosty frown, as if he can't hear her.

"I'm not catching," Eddie's little head says. It's what he said on the phone. His beleaguered eyes dart to me, his smile becoming conspiratorial. He *is* our Olive underneath.

"Who says you wasn't catchin'? I don't know that."

Finesse puts one large hand behind Eddie's scrawny neck, then another low down on his back and moves him upward onto his slab of pillows like a marionette, revealing bony shoulders, more of his small arms, and a bit of emaciated chest and ribs underneath his hospital smock the same bland, green color as hers. "Sit on up," she says irritably. "You all scrunched down. How you s'pose to talk to your friend?" Finesse hasn't looked my way since I came in. Eddie is her lookout. Not me. "You can come on and get close to him," she says—to me— without looking. "He might cough on you, though, so be careful." She has the sponge tucked under her arm.

"I don't remember you being so goddamn tall," Eddie croaks, up on his pillows. He is still monkey-ish. I edge closer without wanting or meaning to. The room is a bedroom. Heavy curtains block the windows. Pale outside light seeps around the edges, turning the air greenish. It's possible to think it's three in the morning, not ten A.M. Eddie has a gooseneck lamp shining onto where he was reading his *Economist*. His bed is cluttered with books, newspapers, Christmas cards, a copy of *Playboy,* a laptop, a plastic player that pipes music to his ear via a wire, but lying unused on the sheet. A tiny, un-majestic, plastic Christmas tree sits on his bed table, something Finesse has no doubt bought at CVS and brought along. Elsewhere on the bed are scattered a bunch of what look like brochures—the top one proposing "Best Buys in

Kolkata"—as if Eddie was planning a trip. Fike, little Christian brigand, has left behind a shiny pamphlet with a red cross on its front above the words "We Appeal to You." I've brought nothing, not even my full self.

"Look at *that* shit," Eddie rasps, his voice clipped and high-pitched after coughing. He's gesturing behind me at two big TVs, bracketed high up, side by side, over the door I just came through and that Finesse is now gliding back out of, saying "Y'all just carry on y'all talkin'. I'll be in here." Both TVs are going but silent. On one, a group of big smiling white men in business suits and cowboy hats is crowded behind the podium of the stock exchange, soundlessly ringing in another day's choker profits and looking blameless. On the other is an aerial view of The Shore. Surf sudsy. Beaches empty. The famous roller coaster, up to its knees in ocean. Somewhere down there my wife is at present counseling grievers. Possibly everything to a dying man is an emblem of the same thing: it's all a lot of shit.

Eddie's commenced coughing again, though he also seems to be laughing. He's shaking his head, trying to talk. "We don't really achieve much clarity, do we, Basset Hound?" His laughter's encountering serious obstacles down deep. "I don't think . . ." (cough, grind, gag, gulp) "that information's . . ." (last laugh attempt, then the deep "Uh-ooo" groan I heard on the phone) " . . . that information's really power, do you?"

"Maybe not. I haven't thought much about it."

"Why *would* you?" Eddie manages. "Everybody knows everything. It's probably better." He subsides back into his bunched pillows and goes silent.

Eddie's the poster boy for death-warmed-over. No one was ever intended to look like Eddie and be breathing—his facial skin gone to parchment, his eyes deep in bony, zombie-sockets, his temples caved. Someone (Finesse) has smeared Vaseline on his clean-shaven cheeks to keep him from what? Drying up? Liquefying? His face glistens evilly. The whole room feels soggy and muggy, the breathable milieu of the soon-to-be-gone. Why did I come here when I could've stayed home, humming Copland and practicing my Narpool? Just because I *could*? That's not good enough.

And where's the mellow-voiced male companion I talked to on the phone? Obviously Finesse has taken his place. I miss him even without knowing him.

On his bed table beside the pathetic plastic Christmas tree, sit cluttered all the odious sick-room implements Eddie needs in order to die better—tissues, a covered metal tray, a silver beaker with a white flexible straw for him to get a sip. Several printed prescription containers. Though there're no resuscitative trappings—no wall defibrillator or electric paddles to stand clear of, no digital gauges to tick off the heart's gradual sink-sink-sink to sayonara. Only a shiny new walker and an empty wheelchair folded into the corner. The patient's not walking out of here in a better frame of mind.

Eddie, however, *has* also dyed his thick hair as black as tar. Though the dye, something else Finesse grabbed at the CVS, has run below Eddie's hairline, making him look even weirder—worse than he's going to look once he breathes his last. At the end, life does not become him.

Strangely—to me, anyway—just beneath the wall TVs hangs a color picture of Smiley Obama, big teeth white as aspirins, elbows faux athletically tight-in to his skinny ribs, bending forward shaking hands with a small, grinning, gray-haired man who used to be Eddie. Behind them hangs a square red-and-gray banner with MIT Entrepreneurs Club For Barack printed on it. I'm sure Fike took it in.

"So." Eddie's staring upward at the blank ceiling. He coughs smally, and with his spectral fingers pulls his sheet closer to his chin, straining the tubing to his hand. Possibly he's practicing being a corpse. "How *are* you, Frank?"

"Pretty good," I say, whispering. Why?

"What're you reading?" Eddie breathes in deeply. A rusty-metal *clank* noise comes out of him, not—it seems—through his mouth.

"I like to read the letters of famous writers," I say. It's true. "I feel like I'm in on an interesting conversation. I'm reading Larkin's letters to his girlfriend. He was an anti-Semite, a racist, and a cad. I find that pretty interesting."

"Uh-huh," Eddie grunts. Not interested. Another small cough. "I got this crud flying through that goddamn volcano ash from London a few years ago. Or, who knows, maybe the goddamn hurricane did it. I don't know. Nothing else makes sense."

I pause. Not likely. "Maybe so."

Eddie moves his small left foot to the side and out from under his bedsheet. The top of his foot is angrified, dried and scrawny—vestigial. He wiggles his toes and raises his head to give a look and re-affiliate with his foot's existence. For some reason—it's an awful thought—I think of Eddie being helped out of his bed in his gaping green smock (to get to the john) and exposing his awful ass and poor, same-sized dick. I would avert my eyes.

"You wrote a book, didn't you?" Eddie returns his scalded foot to the covers' protection.

"A long time ago," I say. "Two. I wrote two. I put the second one in a desk drawer and locked it and burned the desk." Not true but true enough.

"I wonder," Eddie says, his brow and mouth for a moment relaxed. "I always wonder. I was an engineer." The past tense naturally fits the moment. "I wonder, when you write a book, how do you know when you've finished it? Do you know ahead of time? Is that always clear? It baffles me. Nothing I did had an end."

This of course is the question my students used to ask thirty years ago when, for a few fierce months, I taught at a small New England college while my first marriage circled down the drain in the aftermath of our son's death. Why they were interested in that always baffled *me,* since they stood at the bright beginning of their privileged lives, had never finished anything of importance and possibly never would. Eddie is/was (he's both) probably one of those people who wants to know all about everything he's doing at the precise moment he does it. In this case dying.

"Endings always seemed pretty arbitrary to me, Eddie. I wasn't very good at them. I'm not the only person who said so."

Eddie's little raisin eyes move slowly my way behind his smudged glasses. A look of giddy reproach. He is an awful sight—dyed hair, Vaselined cheeks, Jolly Roger smile of doomed intensity. Though he can still cerebrate and feel reproach. "You mean you just stopped when you felt like it?"

"Not exactly. I asked myself if I had anything more to say—if I'd gotten myself fully expressed. And if the answer was yes, I stopped. You bet. But if I didn't, I kept on putting words down."

"Doesn't sound right," Eddie says. He coughs three shallow, staccato gaks, then gropes for a tissue from the box on the bed table. He gaks again and deposits something ungodly into a fold of the tissue, then wipes a bit of it back on his lips.

Probably he's ready to start in again about there being too few people dying, and how we need to do something about it pronto. He's still trying.

I hear Finesse in the next room. She's left the door open to keep tabs on us and is talking on her phone. "I thought he'd come up and get me, okay?" she's saying sternly. "I thought I knew him. But you can't ever think you know nobody. You know what I'm sayin'? I mean, if I'm s'posed to fuck a sixty-year-old man, it's damn sure gon' be my husband. Uh-huh."

Eddie's gaze has wandered back to the TVs. One's tuned to evil-empire Fox. The other, to blandly see-it-your-way CNN. Fox has begun showing the skating rink at Rockefeller Plaza, where half the world is on the ice below a preposterously large and lighted Christmas tree. CNN's rehearsing last weekend's NFL offerings. My sudden fear is that Eddie's literary interest means he's about to hit me up to read something—something he's written—his own memoir, or a "novel" whose central character's an inventor named "Eric." Once you publish a book, even a hundred years back and have lost the sight in both eyes, you're still fair game.

Finesse's big coifed head suddenly appears in the door from the seafaring room. She's holding her red cell phone in her hand. "You all still alive in there? You awful quiet." She looks pityingly in at us. "I don't hear no laughin' and tellin' jokes. You ain't got all serious, have you?" She gives me a mock-serious frown. "I don't want to have to give both you an enema. He done had his. My sister up in Newark says it's a big storm comin' on. I hope neither one of y'all's plannin' a Christmas trip." I am. She disappears again.

"You know, they're not keeping me alive here, Frank," Eddie says—hoarse, his voice strained and boyish. "Hospice doesn't do that. Life just happens or it doesn't. Bravery's not involved. It's interesting. Everybody ought to do it at least once." Eddie's deviled, dyed-hair, Vaseline-smudged face looks shocked, as if he's trying to laugh again, but can only register alarm. "Oh," he manages. "Oh-oh-oh-oh-oh."

"Can I do anything for you, Eddie?" I've inched closer to his bedside but am not inclined to touch him.

"Like what?" Eddie croaks.

"An enema."

Eddie's eyes snap at me. "You'd probably like it."

"Not all of it," I say. "Ole Olive. You've got yourself in a pickle here, haven't you?"

"Do you think so?" Eddie says, his parched lips curled.

Finesse laughs at something her sister in Newark has had to say. "I was never a good sleeper, anyway," she says and laughs raucously.

Eddie takes a deep clattering breath. Each one of these could be his last. Eddie could pop off as dead as a mallet with me standing here pointless, hardly knowing him. "Mr.

Medley expired while joking with an unidentified man about enemas."

Audible outside the house, across the soggy, puddly grounds of *casa* Eddie, comes the lonely *ping-ping-ping* and guttural heave 'n' hump of a heating oil truck. Skillman's— I've seen it when driving over. It's making a delivery, possibly to this very domicile. I hope my Sonata's not in the way when the driver starts backing up without looking.

"You know"—Eddie gulps hard and dry and thin—"all this shit you think you can't live with. Colostomy bag. Vegetative state. Commandant at Bergen-Belsen. You can live with anything. The mind just goes back to a previous state."

"Maybe *that's* enough clarity," I say, beside his bed.

"Yeah. Maybe." Eddie breathes again almost easily. For a moment, he seems less under subversive attack, as if his brain had struck a truce with his body's assailants. Maybe my being here is a benefaction. A very bad smell now escapes from under Eddie's covers. No telling what. "What I can't live with— it's awful to say. Awful to *know*. I realize I won't ever pass a woman in a revolving door and have her look at me in that way. You know? That's over. It's shameful to say that. Every productive thing I ever did came from that feeling. I know it about myself." Eddie fiddles up under his sheet with the hand not tubed up to the drip bag. "Ohhhh," he moans and averts his face in recognition of whatever he's come into contact with down there. A catheter or some equally monstrous intrusion on his person. So many things can go wrong, it's strange any go right. I'm thinking maybe two miniature Vietnamese masseuses—a mercy flight from KumWow—might offer Eddie a better send-off than I'm managing; affirm his faith that life happens 'til it doesn't. Finesse wouldn't mind.

"It's not shameful, Eddie," I say, relative to the origin of his species. "Everything comes from someplace."

"I have to tell you something, Frank," Eddie says quickly, his chest expanding under his blue sheet, as if he's trying to suppress a new onslaught.

"That's what I'm here for." Not literally true. Eddie may mistake me for the angel of death, and this moment his last try at coherence. Death makes of everything in life a dream.

"I have to get this out of my head. I don't want to die being driven crazy by it. I might as well not die."

"Give me your worst, Eddie." Wise to keep all responses to a minimum. Locate my Default Self. It doesn't matter what I say anyway. Eddie and I are of one mind—life is a matter of subtractions.

Finesse again leans into the doorway, gives us another look of worried but mock disapproval. "Y'all ain't no fun." She fattens her cheeks as if she's disgusted. Eddie and I might as well be one person.

"I fucked Ann." Eddie's staring straight up—fiercely—

out of his vanquished, soon-to-be-untenanted body, his ghastly beady eyes unblinking behind his specs, in their hollow, bony sockets, the tops of which have black hair-dye encroaching.

At least, I *believe* that's what Eddie's just said. His stricken face indicates he *thinks* he said something important.

"What?" I could've heard him wrong. Neither of us is talking very loud. Then in case I'm right, I say, *"When?"*

Eddie lets go with an immense cough—a bottom scraper. This time he covers his mouth and emits a groan. For a moment he seems incapable of speaking and purses his gunked lips like a zipper.

"What?" I say again, still not very loud, but pushing in a little closer.

Eddie clears his throat and makes an awful gasping-gurgling noise, then very fast says, "You-were-away-teaching-someplace-in-Mass. It-wasn't-that-long-after-your-son-died-she-was-alone—Jalina-had-left. Uhhhhgh. I'm sorry. I'm really sorry. I was careless."

"What?" I say a third time. "When I was . . . teaching? You fucked Ann?" A pause. "My Ann?" Another pause. "Why'd you do that?"

It isn't so much I'm saying these words as much as they're being vocalized *through* me. I hear them when Eddie does.

"I can't put the genie back in the bottle now, Frank." Eddie gulps, then gurgles, then averts his head as if he wants to recede into the deathly air, like the specter he'll soon be. Outside, the Skillman Oil truck's commencing its large liquid infusion. Durning, durning, durning, through the house pipes, into a cast receptacle. "I fell in love with her, Frank," Eddie's strangled voice manages, his monkey face still staring away. "I wanted her to live with me in France. In Deauville. Take her on my boat. She said no. She loved you. I don't want to die with that deception as my legacy. I'm so sorry." Eddie heaves. Pain, sob—what's the difference?

"Why . . ." I'm about to say something I'm not really sure about the nature of. *Why* have you told me this? *Why* should I believe you? *Why* would this come up now—when your last breaths are prizable and should be saved for prizable utterances? *Why* would I want to hear this? I'm looking down at poor Eddie. What my face portrays I don't know. What *should* it portray? It's possible I have no words or feelings for what Eddie's just told me. Which is satisfactory.

"You-two-were-almost-divorced, Frank," Eddie says speedily, as if my hands were around his neck. They aren't.

"Well," I say, and pause and think a moment, back through the years. "That's not exactly true, Eddie." I am immensely, imperturbably calm. A calm with few words. "We *did* get divorced. That's true. But we weren't *almost* divorced. We were married. That's the wrong order. Time goes the other way. Or it used to."

"I know," Eddie croaks. "You and I didn't know each other that well, Frank." Again, the clattery, clunking fireplace-grate noises deep in Eddie's breathing machinery—unidentifiable except as fatal.

"No," I say. No, that's right. No, you're wrong. No, perhaps now's the time for your last breath.

I have recently developed a tiny groove in the rear of my lower right canine, something my night guard should protect me against but of course doesn't. My tongue finds it now and scours it until there's a leakage of rich tongue blood I can taste. I also feel slight pelvic-pain heat below-decks. I'd like to get the fuck out of here; maybe stand outside and have a word in the driveway with Ezekiel Lewis, driver of the Skillman truck and scion of a long line of Haddam Lewises, stretching beyond last century's mists, when their great-great-grandfather Stand-Off Lewis came up from Dixie accompanying a stalwart young white seminarian as his valet. And, naturally, stayed. I once employed Ezekiel's father, Wardell, when I was in the realty business. They are our heritage here. We are their spoiled legacy. If I had one black friend in town, him or her I'd keep. There'd be plenty of laughing involved. Not this kind of tired, tiresome, unhappy, deathbed shit I'm putting up with at the moment. White people's shit. No wonder we're disappearing. We're over-bred. Our genie's out of its bottle.

"Tell me what you think of me, Frank." Eddie's regard wants to come back to me, but gets claimed by the two TVs high on the wall. Fox has loser Romney, addressing a convention of habited nuns, beaming as if he'd just won something. CNN has a smiling Andy Williams, who, it seems, has sadly died. Both—dead and alive—seek our approval.

But is this all that life comes down to when you take away damn near everything? What do you think of me? Tell me, tell me, *tell me!* My wife said the same thing to me just days ago. It must be grief not to know.

"It doesn't change anything, Olive," I say, not sure what I could mean by that. It's just the truest thing I can say. Maybe Eddie would like me to give him a punch in the nose on his deathbed. (What would Finesse think of *that?*) But I'm not mad—at anyone. A wound you don't feel is not a wound. Time fixes things, mostly.

"I'm an insomniac, Frank," Eddie says and coughs shallowly, fading eyes still on the TVs—which one I can't be sure. Mitt or Andy. "Things get in my head and won't go away."

"Most insomniacs sleep more than they think they do, Eddie." I take a step back from his bed. I'm departing. We both are.

Eddie's cell phone on the bed starts ringing with a tune. *What good is sit-ting a-lone in your room, come hear the muuu-sic play . . .*

"I'm dying and the fucking phone rings," Eddie says, his wraith's hand clutching, fumbling through the bedclothes. He smiles at me gratefully, venomously. "Lemme get this. If I can. Sorry." He gasps and squeezes his weary eyes shut to be able to speak.

"Go for it, Olive." I raise my hand like an Indian brave.

"Eddie Medley," I hear him say, hoarse, high-pitched, evanescent. "Who's this? Hello!"

Start by ad-mit-ting from crad-le to tomb is-n't that long a stay . . .

I'm gone.

Outside, in late-December late-morning spring, it's hard to believe that in one day's time all will be white and Christmas-y, and I will be on a sentimental journey to the nation's midsection. My son and I will have some laughs, crack some corny jokes, see a great river and the Great Plains' commencement, eat some top KC sirloin, possibly visit Hallmark and the house of Thomas Hart Benton (a favorite of mine), and talk long into the night about rent-to-own. If I can only get there.

The two scolding crows have exited their branch in the beech tree. I hear them not far away in another yard, other things on their minds. Given all, I'm feeling surprisingly good about this day, with much of it still to come. The taste of blood in my mouth has vanished.

"*All* right now, *all* right . . ." A voice I know—Ezekiel's—coming round the side of Eddie's deteriorating house, ready to slide the fuel bill under the door, as he does at my house. " . . . Christmas gift!" he sings out and smiles at me as if I'm a fixture out here on the pea gravel, no different from the Henry Moore bronze.

"Christmas gift," I say back in the old southern way. Though he's as Jersey as they come. Ezekiel is a strapping, smiling, shaved-head, spiritual dynamo in his green Skillman jumpsuit. We "go back" without having to know each other all that well or be friends. White southerners all think we "know" Negroes better than we do or could. They may think they know us, too—with better reason. Ezekiel, though, is good on any scale of human goodness. He is thirty-nine, attends the AME Tabernacle over in the black trace, coaches wrestling at the Y, teaches Sunday School, volunteers at the food bank. His wife, Be'ahtrice, teaches high school math and knows the universal sign language. He is bedrock. The best we have to offer.

Off, streets away, I hear again the bells of St. Leo gong-gonging out carols for the spiritually wavering. "Doesn't feel much like Christmas," I say.

"If you don't like the weather . . ." Ezekiel's going past me, smiling as if he has a secret.

" . . . just wait ten minutes," I say. He is as fully expressed as anyone I know. "Are you heading for a big holiday, Mr. Lewis?" I say, standing by my still-warm car, taking him admiringly in.

"Oh, yeah. Count my blessings." He's bending to slip the yellow card under the door bottom. Eddie will never see it. Ezekiel is a huge man, though dainty in his practiced movements. "Our church's taking a panel truck of food and whatever over to those people sufferin' on The Shore. Cain't do that much. But I'm here. So I cain't do nothin'." He's headed back toward me in the sunny morning.

"That's right," I say. It is. I will think on it more. Time fixes things, but it is also short, and precious.

"I started taking Spanish lessons at the Y," Ezekiel says. A trace of heating oil scent accompanies him, his big, soiled workman's gloves in his hand. "Be'ahtrice and I are both doin' it. There's a church over in Asbury. A lot of 'em don't even speak our language. How they gon' make out?" He's nodding, his cheeks partly inflated by thought. Christmas is serious to him. An opportunity. Heating oil is secondary.

We're unexpectedly, then, trapped in the instant—too much sudden seriousness. We fall silent. Though he smiles at me in recognition. I smile back. It becomes for us a moment to know the expanding largeness of it all.

"How's your son Ralph, Mr. Bascombe?" He means my son Paul. They knew each other long ago in school. It is a sweetness that brings tears to my eyes.

"He's fine, Ezekiel. He's just fine. I'll tell him you asked."

"Is he still . . ." Ezekiel looks at me oddly. He's sensed his mistake and is transfixed. It is the finest of fine with me.

"He *is,*" I say. "He's still in Kansas City. He runs a garden supply out there." I touch my fingertip to my eye's corner.

"He was always good with that," Ezekiel says,

"He was," I lie.

"All right then." Ezekiel's moving. "Santa's gotta get on back to his sleigh and be flyin'.'"

"You do that," I say. He shakes my hand in his large, amazingly soft one. That is what we have a chance to say to each other on Christmas Eve. A few good words.

Then he goes. And I go. The day we have briefly shared is saved.

ACKNOWLEDGMENTS

My thanks to my great friend Daniel Halpern for encouraging the writing of this book. My thanks to my dear one Amanda Urban for being this book's advocate, and mine. My thanks, as well, to the wonderful Dale Rohrbaugh for invaluable and resourceful help. My thanks, also, to Laurie McGee, the best copy editor a boy could have. And thanks to Eleanor Kriseman for precious assistance in many phases of this book's life.

My thanks to Janet Henderson for long conversations over time, which vitally informed one of the stories here. My thanks to the Gros Morne Summer Music artists for playing Copland for me in Newfoundland. My thanks to my friend Philip Levine for his knowledge of obdurate pigs.

Several friends who inspired and affected this book's origins have sadly departed and are sorely missed: Holly Eley, whom I thank for her great wit; Jeff Levin, whom I thank for his refinements, humor, and ingenuity; Bill Wyman, for his dear affection.

I also thank my lifelong friend Charlie Scott for being exemplary in life. And I thank most of all Kristina Ford for her countless grace notes.

—RF